GODLESS

A BLOODLINES NOVEL

SLMN

 Kingston Imperial

CHAPTER
ONE

The truck charged towards the compound, engine shrieking, gears howling, tires spitting grit and dirt, powering towards the fortified gates at ramming speed. The barriers were built to keep out anyone who did not belong to the Awon Woli.

It had begun as a dust cloud heading in his direction, but something about it wasn't right, so Daudi M'Beki raised the alarm. He'd been joined on the ramparts by three other men. Each of them clutched an automatic rifle, muzzle trained on the truck. All four of them were killers. They wouldn't hesitate to squeeze the trigger and end the lives of everyone in that runaway truck if it tried to breach the compound. No questions.

The truck came closer and closer, showing no sign of stopping. The distance and the dust made it impossible to tell if it was one of their own. If it was, their man was returning with the hounds of hell on his tail.

The Awon Woli had been driven out of their own country by civil war—and unlike the 'legitimate' businessmen who exploited genocide for gain, they'd seen their own opportunities reduced to the point where their survival was seriously in jeopardy.

They weren't far from the border.

They'd worked hard to keep supply lines open, but at a cost.

The Awon Woli remained vigilant. On edge. Prepared for the inevitable escalation when it came. There were plenty who wanted them out and would go to any length to see them in the ground rather than let them live in peace.

Looking at the dust storm behind the truck it was hard not to think that the time to die had come, finally.

Daudi was the youngest of the four on the ramparts, but he was ready. Death held no fear. The butt of his rifle dug into his shoulder. His finger rested over the trigger. His hands were slick with sweat. Heat haze shimmered between him and the truck.

He didn't blink.

"We wait," he said.

They had an understanding; whoever had been on watch decided when it was time to fire. It made it easier than arguing about authority and power.

"Until we see the whites of the dead man's eyes," one of the others laughed.

It was Razi, one of the young guys who were obsessed with old films. They'd found rusted cans filled with reels of them and watched them at night on a rusty old projector. There was an irony to the original line that he didn't get; it had been used to decide when the white soldiers pull the trigger to execute the oncoming black men.

"On my mark," Daudi said, ignoring his companion.

He knew that he would have to make the call soon or it would be too late to stop the vehicle from crashing into the gates. And without knowing if it was friend or foe he was executing.

He breathed deeply, keeping his heart rate steady. The slightest rush of blood could have the bullet veering wide of the mark, the markings from this distance were very slight.

He was ready.

His lips parted, ready to give the word, but the truck suddenly braked and slewed sideways spitting even more dust as the driver executed a handbrake turn. He saw a broken taillight.

Something was thrown from the back of the truck and then it was thundering away again.

Daudi lowered his weapon. The threat was gone. The dust slowly settled around a dark shape on the makeshift road.

"What the fuck is that?" Razi asked, slowly lowering his own weapon.

Daudi knew what it was.

What he didn't know was *who* it was.

"Keep watch, he said, then gestured for one of the others to follow him down from their vantage point.

———

There were other people moving around the compound. There were questions, but most of them just carried on with what they were doing.

Daudi called, "Open the gate."

He moved quickly towards it. The rusted iron hinges protested. The bottom edge dragged across the ground in a wail of metal. He wore the black armband that marked him as watch leader. That was enough to give him the authority to bark orders and expect them to be carried out without question.

"What the fuck is going on out here?" a voice behind him demanded.

Daudi turned, knowing who the voice belonged to.

The hulk of a man had emerged from the central building in the compound. He was known to all of them as Boss. No more, no less. Boss. It wasn't that there weren't those amongst them who knew his real name, it had just lost any sort of meaning, and Boss liked it that way.

"There's someone out there," Daudi said.

"One of ours?"

"Maybe."

Boss waved him away. "Go," he said, motioning for one of the men who'd emerged from the building with him to follow Daudi out of the compound. It was another big man, this one mysteriously named Gentle when he was anything but.

Daudi would rather have done this without Boss standing over him, especially as he'd let the truck get so close to the compound, and then let it race away without firing a single shot.

It made them look weak, and in this life, perception was everything.

Outside, there was no mistaking the shape on the ground, or the fact that it was already dead.

There was nothing to be gained by rushing, but that didn't stop him from running to it.

Boss wouldn't want him wasting time.

The body was face down in the dirt, his hands bound behind his back with cable ties. There was a plastic bag over his head.

Daudi paused for a moment and took another breath to steady himself. It was long enough for the other man to come up alongside him.

"What are you waiting for?" Gentle said, then crouched down and turned the body over. It didn't help. The plastic was smeared with red, making it impossible to make out the features of the face inside.

Daudi tried to rip the plastic open, but couldn't get a decent purchase, so he fumbled in his pocket for a knife.

"Leave it, we need to get him inside," Gentle told him, ignoring the armband that should have meant Daudi was the one giving the orders. "I don't like the idea of us being exposed like this when those fuckers can do something like this to one of our own. Watch my back."

The big man lifted the body in his arms as if it was no weight at all and set off at an easy run back towards the open gates.

Daudi unslung his weapon and held it the ready, walking backwards toward the compound, scanning the open ground in an arc.

There was no sign of movement out there.

That didn't matter.

He wasn't about to drop his guard when a bullet could drop him before he blinked.

He glanced over his shoulder and saw that Gentle and his burden had already slipped through the gate. With them inside, he turned and ran.

CHAPTER
TWO

They burned the body the next day, well outside the compound, using a patch of scrubland.

Daudi had watched Gentle use the tip of a machete to delicately split open the plastic bag over the body's head. His view had been obscured as others gathered around, close. Blood oozed rather than ran, thick and dark. They had to wash the dead man's face before they could be sure who it was.

"Lebna," one of the others said and there was a murmur of agreement that rippled through the gathering.

"Send word to his father," Boss said, but no one seemed keen to break the news to him. Eventually, Boss took it out of their hands and nodded for a chosen messenger to go. The man peeled away from the crowd and set off at a run. Daudi could not take his eyes off the blood-smeared face.

Lebna had been missing for a couple of weeks.

Everyone knew he'd met some girl in town and had been planning to set up house with her. Boss hadn't been too concerned; he hadn't tried to stop him, which surprised a few of us, but most of them knew that Lebna would be welcomed back with open arms when he chose to return. That was how Boss ran the compound. They weren't prisoners. No one had imagined his return would be like this.

Boss squatted on his haunches beside the boy. He rubbed a thumb across Lebna's cheek. "They cut his tongue out," he said, quietly at first, and then it came out as a roar. "They cut his fucking tongue out!"

He got to his feet just as Lebna's father came hobbling towards the crowd.

He was not an old man, but a gunshot wound to his left leg had caused damage that would never be repaired.

"Who could do this?" he wailed. "Who would do something like this?"

"The Onisagbe," Daudi said, knowing it was the truth, even without evidence. A few faces turned in his direction as if he had dared speak the unspeakable.

Who else could it be?

"Perhaps," said Boss, fixing him with a steely stare. "Perhaps if you had stopped them, or at least given the order before they fled like the cowards they are, we might know that by now."

Boss placed a hand on the shoulder of the bereaved father, showing him a moment of compassion. "We will have our revenge on whoever did this," he said. "You have my word. We won't just take out one of theirs, there will be no simple eye for an eye. We will find the man who held the knife and do the same to him; this is about justice, not simple revenge. In the meantime, whoever was on duty with Daudi, start gathering wood to build a funeral pyre, even if you have to work through the night. It's only right that a father should have a night to say goodbye to his son."

Daudi knew that he should have done better; he should have made the call to shoot. They should have riddled the Onisagbe truck with bullets and left the bastards bleeding in the dirt right alongside Lebna.

He motioned for the others who had been with him on the ramparts to follow him back out through the gate, filled with shame.

He knew where the funeral pyre needed to be built and they would do it without complaint.

It would take Daudi a long time to redeem himself.

If he ever could.

The sky remained free of cloud and the light of the moon was enough that they could do their work quickly, three of them working while the fourth kept an eye out for potential threats, rotating the roles to ensure they all shared the work. But Daudi cut and carried word without a break. It was his penance even if the Boss hadn't demanded it and wouldn't see it.

They moved Lebna's body from where it had lain, but even in the moonlight Daudi could make out the darker patch in the dirt. It would be kicked over and washed away for the next few days, but he would always remember where it had been.

He wished that his guilt was as easily washed away.

He would not forget the look on Lebna's face, his father's anguish, or the blood.

He owed them both vengeance, whatever Boss said. Justice. Vengeance. It was just semantics. They both meant the same thing. He owed them both a body.

CHAPTER
THREE

The music was pumping. The lights pulsed in time. A lone woman danced on the floor. Everyone in the club knew that it would be a dumb idea to go and join her without an explicit invitation, and even then, it wasn't exactly smart for a guy to take up that invitation.

Most men watched and hoped she appreciated their admiration from afar.

Dana Danjuma, daughter of Sol Danjuma, the Onisagbe's chief, and more importantly, the man who ran Freetown, could have any of the men in the room if she wanted them, and she knew it. Just as easily she could have had them killed, if the whim struck her. Both were a kind of death sentence as far as her father was concerned, but that didn't stop her from playing. Once she was done with them, her playthings were better off disappearing if they didn't want to be disappeared.

Dana could be every bit as cold as her father with people who didn't matter to her, but fiercely loyal to those who did..

Sol Danjuma was in the club that night, too. He sat at his usual table on the upper landing, surveying the dancefloor and everything else he owned. It was noisier than he liked, but there were people he wanted to meet. People from out of town who had come looking to do business with him. They'd insisted on the public meeting. This was public.

It was good that they were afraid of him, but if they had done their due diligence, they should have known that nowhere was safe for them in Freetown if he made the call.

He'd been at the table for ten minutes when they arrived.

"You have the money?" Danjuma said.

This was not something for nothing.

The man put a battered attaché case on the table next to the pristine suitcase. He opened it to show the bundles of US currency, all of it well thumbed. "Do you want to count it?"

Danjuma snorted again. "If the money is short, you will be dead before you can get out of Freetown," he said. "I'm assuming you are fond of life."

"We are."

"Good. And besides, I know you don't want this to be a one-off arrangement. Stands to reason, given the trouble you've gone to, to get in front of me."

Danjuma nodded for his bodyguard to open the suitcase and in the process reveal a number of packages of white powder. "Do you want to sample the merchandise?"

He enjoyed the other man's uncertainty. There was no mistaking the nervous glance he gave to his silent companion.

"It's fine," he said, after a heartbeat. "What is a relationship without trust?"

"Indeed," Sol Danjuma agreed.

The man got his feet and held out a hand.

Danjuma looked at it for a moment, his expression one of measured distaste, as though he was looking at shit stains where the man had just wiped his ass with it.

For a moment it seemed he wasn't going to accept it and seal their pact.

But then he got to his feet and grasped the man's hand in a powerful shake, pulling him in. The man didn't flinch, but Danjuma savored the pain in his eyes. He released his grip before it became unbearable. He'd made his point, asserted his dominance. That was enough.

He sank back down into his chair and returned to watching his daughter dance—or more accurately, the men who hungered for her, knowing she was unattainable, the forbidden fruit. He ignored the two men who had come to buy the cocaine.

By the time he next took his eyes from the dancefloor they were gone, as was his righthand man, along with the money they had brought in offering. He could forget about business for the rest of the evening. He gestured for the waitress to bring another Chivas.

He watched his daughter dance.

The music stopped for a moment and Dana smile up at him. She gave a little wave. He returned it with a smile and a moment later she had called another couple of young women up onto the dance floor to join her.

It made him smile to see her enjoying herself. He was happy to see her grown into the beautiful young woman she had become, so like her mother. But it would be a blessing from the gods if her younger sister decided not to cause him quite so much trouble. Sol Danjuma chuckled at the thought, knowing there was more chance of penguins turning up in hell. Lori might have been 14, but it was painfully obvious to anyone with eyes to see that she was going to be trouble.

CHAPTER
FOUR

Joseph Connors sat in the car with the suitcase on his lap.

He had no intention of letting go of it.

He'd already done things he would never have dreamed of doing even a week ago to get his chance at the big time. This was it. This was everything and more. All he had to do was get the merchandise across the Atlantic and he would be home.

Which made it sound easy.

It wasn't.

It was anything but, but he'd done the background work. He knew the traffic well. He knew the routes, what went along what lines, and who controlled them. He had a route planned that was going to take him places where the authorities wouldn't be looking for large consignments of drugs. It was all about planning. Risk takers got caught. He wasn't a risk taker. He was a thoughtful planner. Methodical.

And if things went tits up, he had the perfect fall guy sitting right next to him.

Travis served many purposes. He was the driver. He was the hired muscle paid to look good and when the need arose, get his hands dirty. And he was the fall guy.

"Surprisingly painless," Travis noted, eyes not leaving the road.

There wasn't much in the way of traffic on the road. They moved toward the outskirts of town. The plan was simple. As few moving parts as possible. That was the way Connors liked to work. First, return to their flea-pit hovel of a hotel they'd rented a room at for the last couple of nights. Crash, then head out in the morning, and get the fuck out of here while the fucking was good. Travis had argued the benefits of hitting the road straight away, do not pass go, do not collect two hundred bucks, but Connors wasn't running. It was about perception. He didn't want that bastard Danjuma thinking they were frightened of him. Stay, rest, project an air of confidence. One of the benefits of getting into bed with the devil was his aura of protection extended to them now.

No one was going to touch them.

"Your reasoning?" Connors asked.

"We were outnumbered, outgunned, and in his backyard. If he'd got it into his head to take the money and stiff us on the merchandise, there was not a single fucking thing we could have done. There was nothing 'public' about that meet. You count how many of the people in there were Danjuma's?"

"Four of five," Connors said, but he knew that he was guessing.

"Twice that, if not more. Our luck held. We shouldn't push it. We aren't always going to have his daughter to run interference."

"His daughter?"

Another glance. "Shit, man, are you telling me you didn't even notice *her*? Lord preserve us from blind men who think they can see. She was cutting up the dancefloor all on her lonesome, while half the jaws in the place were on the floor."

"You weren't supposed to be looking at the pretty girls on the dancefloor, you were there to look out for me."

"I wasn't watching her; I was assessing threat levels. I can't protect you if I don't know who is where. Danjuma had enough people there to put us in the ground as easily as he ordered that drink, a wave of the fucking hand. His daughter being there might just have saved our lives. No one wants to look like a monster in front of their little girl, even a man like Danjuma, who is willing to pay a premium for someone like me to take care of his little problem when it relates to one of those girls."

"You think?"

"Educated guess. Taking into consideration everything I've heard about the man. We got lucky. I don't like relying on luck."

They fell silent.

The car slowed as they reached their hotel.

Connors waited for Travis to get out before he opened his door.

He knew that they were safe enough from anyone apart from Danjuma, of course. Travis had put that doubt in his mind and it wasn't going anywhere. If he couldn't kill them on the dance floor, what was to stop him from doing it the moment they were out of the club? This was his city. He could have had them followed, or knowing where they were based, have someone waiting for them to show up.

He'd watched for headlights behind them as they drove through Freetown but hadn't marked anything suspicious or out of place. That didn't mean they weren't out to get them, though. Travis was right.

How easily the euphoria of the moment blew away on the African wind.

Maybe Travis was right about more stuff. Maybe it would have been the smart play to just drive, abandon the shit in the hotel, and just go.

The only problem was his passport was in his suitcase.

And the suitcase was on one of those metal racks beside the TV.

"Okay. I'm thinking maybe you're right, we grab our stuff and go, no looking back," he said, still clutching the case as he clambered out of the passenger seat.

Travis locked the car.

"If we get as far as our room, we'll be safe enough," Travis said.

Connors nodded. He scanned the parking lot nervously. It would have been well lit if half the lamps hadn't burned out. He kept close to Travis, more than happy to use the other man as a human shield. His heart beat faster than he could remember it ever beating before. His gaze darted every which way, trying to take in every angle at once.

"For fuck's sake, man, just act naturally," Travis gruffed. Unlike Connors, he'd only needed one quick look-see to decide they were safe. "Are you trying to let the world know we've got shit in that case of yours they might want to take from us? Take a fucking breath."

Connors did as he was told, not appreciating the irony of how quickly their roles had reversed.

He wasn't in charge of the situation.

He was completely in the hands of the man who was there to protect him.

It wasn't a pleasant revelation.

But by the time they got to the room, Connors was back to wondering why he'd let the other man's paranoia get under his skin.

"You should get some sleep," Travis said as Connors slumped onto his bed.

"Sleep? Not happening. Too much adrenalin pumping through my blood, man. And there's no way I'm taking my eyes of this shit. Not when things can still go very fucking wrong."

Travis shrugged. "Your prerogative. Want me to look after it?"

"No," he said a little too sharply.

Travis raised a hand to save him from having to explain himself. "It's all good. I'll have the seat; I don't need to sleep. But you really should." Travis sank down onto the battered-looking sofa, avoiding some of the more suspicious stains, and put his gun on the seat beside him.

Connors took the bottle of scotch from the nightstand. When he'd stashed it, he'd figured it would be for the inevitable celebration, but instead twisting off the cap was all about calming his frayed nerves.

He offered the other man the bottle after he'd taken two deep swallows.

Travis declined.

CHAPTER
FIVE

Daudi had watched as the funeral pyre was lit at dawn.

Everyone from the compound was present to witness it, even those who had been on watch all night. No one was sleeping. The pile of wood they'd gathered didn't seem as impressive as they'd thought the night before, but the addition of a gallon of petrol splashed all across it was enough to turn it into a blaze.

There was a single moment when he saw through the conflagration to glimpse the body being consumed, and he wished that he hadn't seen it. There was already too much going on inside his head that had no place being in there.

They ate together while the last embers of the fire burned out. A shared meal was a rare event given how many of them there were. A small group had been chosen to disperse the ashes, but the wind was doing most of the job for them.

At the end of the meal, Boss cleared his throat and rose.

"As much as it pains me, we must remember we cannot be sure who killed our brother, whatever our suspicions," he began, "but one incontrovertible truth we *do* know is that he met his death in Freetown. Now, if any of you know the identity of his mystery woman I want to know. Now."

"Surely it has to be the Onisagbe," someone muttered.

"That is not sure. Perhaps Lebna was unlucky, and some love rival wanted him gone? Or maybe he crossed them in some other way? There are alternatives."

"They knew he was one of us," the objection came from down the table.

"No great challenge," Boss said, lifting his shirt to reveal the huge tattoo on his chest. "When we all carry this mark on our body somewhere."

Even without thinking, Daudi's hand went to his upper arm where his own tattoo was etched in his skin. He was pretty sure that Lebna's was in the same place, meaning it couldn't be seen without taking his shirt off.

"I'm not telling any of you where you can and cannot go," Boss said. "You are grown men. You know the risks. As long as you are here when I call on you, I couldn't give a shit what you do in your own time. I have no interest in who you are fucking. But if any of you bring trouble to our gates there will be consequences."

"But what about Lebna? We can't let his death go without *consequences*."

"Don't worry. Something will be done, but not until we're ready. Not until we're sure."

Daudi had no intention of waiting. He needed to feel like he was doing something.

And he had a free day ahead of him.

He thought about returning to his bunk for an hour when they'd finished clearing away the meal. It was still too early to head into town to talk to strangers, but maybe there was someone in the camp who could tell him something? It didn't matter how little; there was no telling what might point him in the right direction.

Zoob had been Lebna's watch partner. If anyone knew his secrets, it would be him. If you spent enough long cold nights on the watch platforms with someone, you ended up talking. Most of it was inevitably bullshit about the things they would do when they were finally able to head home. Who you were going to fuck or fuck up. Daudi had had plenty of those conversations himself, even though he knew they would never be able to go home. That other place was a nice dream, but this was the only home he had known. A fly-blown patch of land outside of civilization. Yesterday, the wind carried dust. Today it brought the ashes of the dead.

Was it really so bad back in their own country that this place was better?

Daudi found Zoob in his bunk.

"How you doin'?" Daudi asked. "Can't be easy."

Zoob shrugged. It was an expressive gesture for a skinny kid. He was barely 16, if that. Unlike Lebna, he had no family in the compound. His story was similar to so many of the others, loved ones either dead or left behind, which amounted to the same thing. "Did you know him?" The boy asked. It was a dumb question; everyone knew everyone in this place.

"Sure," he admitted. "We chatted a few times, drew an extra shift one night when we first came here. Not what I'd call close friends, but we were good."

The boy nodded.

"Has Boss talked to you about him yet?"

"Boss? Why would he want to talk to *me*? I ain't no one to talk to." He was suddenly nervous, fidgeting on his bunk. The body language was easy enough to read; he was making himself smaller, pressing himself into the corner.

"Hey man, it's all good, trust me, nothing to worry about. He'll just want to know anything you can tell him about the girl Lebna was fucking."

That didn't seem to put him at ease. "He said she was beautiful, way out of his league, but that they'd fallen in love."

"Ain't that always the way. You know her name?"

He shook his head. "Naw. I asked him, but he never told me. Said it was too hot to be sharin'. For a while, I figured he was bullshittin' and there was no girl. He was that kinda guy, you know? Talked a good game. I figured he went into town sat in a bar nursing a beer, then came back with a smile on his face."

"Really? And you still think he was full of shit?"

"Naw. Not anymore. He still wouldn't tell me her name, but he told me he was renting an apartment above a launderette. Not them, him. They couldn't put it in her name, he said, too big a risk."

"Okay, now I'm interested," Daudi said, "Anything else you can tell me about it?" But the boy only shrugged. Thinking on his feet, Daudi figured there couldn't be more than a handful of places over launderettes in Freetown. The question was: did he go on his own or take someone with him? Actually, that was only one of the questions, the other one was: should he talk to Boss before he did anything they might not live to regret?

He needed to think.

He left Zoob in peace and headed for his own bunk.

There was no guarantee that he would get peace there, of course.

The last twelve hours had made people sink inside themselves. He moved through the compound without so much as a nod of acknowledgment until he was in the bunk rooms where the single men slept.

Musa lay on his bunk, directly beneath Daudi's own.

He rolled onto his side when he saw Daudi approach.

He wasn't like the others; he would want to talk.

"You okay?" Daudi asked, earning a nod.

"You?"

"Been worse."

"Which translates to been a fuck of a lot better, am I right?"

"You're not wrong."

It was a ritual exchange. Despite everything, it brought a smile to his face. "So, what's on your mind?"

"Just been talking to Zoob," Daudi said, and just like that Musa's eyes came alight, though Daudi wasn't sure if it was with fear or excitement, or maybe a hint of both.

"You crazy? Why've you been talking to him. You know that Boss will find out."

"Nothing to find out. Was just paying my respects," he said.

"Of course you were, blood. And what did your *respects* find out? Don't bullshit me, my friend, I know that look in your eye."

Daudi told him the little he'd been able to learn, all the while glancing around to be sure no one was listening. He didn't want word getting back to Boss before he'd decided what he was going to do, and ideally not until long after he'd actually done it.

"So, who are you going to tell about it?" he asked.

"No one," he said, making his mind up. He knew what he had to do. He had fucked up by not stopping the men who'd dumped Lebna's body. Amends meant putting a name on who'd done that to him. And that began with the mystery girl.

She was the key.

Find her, find the truth.

CHAPTER SIX

Danjuma looked over his coffee cup at his oldest daughter; she looked tired, but more than that, she looked sad. He hated to see her in pain. But he would just have to live with it, play the part of the concerned father, try to offer hope.

"Are you sure you haven't seen him, Dad?" Dana asked

"I didn't see you missing him last night," he said.

She shrugged. "I can forget anything when I'm dancing, it's not real. But when the music stops," she shrugged, and it was the most expressive gesture in the world. It conveyed just how much the world weighed down on her.

"It's only been a couple of days since you last saw him, right? He's a man. He could be out working? On an errand for someone? He could be drunk in a gutter. A couple of days is no time."

"He's not answering his phone. He wouldn't go anywhere without at least letting me know what he was doing."

"Are you sure? I mean, you've barely known him for five minutes."

She shook her head. "You know that's not true," she said. "We've been talking about spending the rest of our lives together."

A grim thought and a dark line flashed through his brain, but Sol Danjuma resisted letting it become words, but it was hard to keep the smile off his face. He hoped that he was gone for good, and she would find someone better. "I'm sure he'll turn up."

"I'm going to call round to his apartment," she said. "I need to see if he's there," which filtered through her beautiful insecurities meant 'I need to see if he's ignoring me.'

"I can send one of my men," he said.

"No," she said. "I need to do this myself."

He played on her weaknesses, "And if he's there? If it turns out he's been hiding from your calls and doesn't want to see you? What then?"

"He wouldn't do that," she said, but it was hard to be sure who she was trying to convince.

"Maybe not, but do you really want to put yourself through that? What's to say he hasn't just cleared out? It's not like there's much tying him to this place."

"Apart from me," Dana said. And for any man in the world that would be enough. Sol Danjuma knew that. "I know you mean well, but... I get it," he said.

"Butt out, dad."

She didn't smile at that. She was close to tears. Words weren't going to fix her. He was going to have to let her do this in her own time, her own way. She'd find the boy, or she'd forget him.

Danjuma was saved from having to feign concern for a minute longer when Lori entered the room. It was rare for the three of them to spend time together and he was glad for this moment, knowing that it wouldn't last because it never did.

"Hey, Sis, what's up?" Lori dropped into the chair beside Dana.

Despite the age difference, and the fact they had different mothers, both deceased, the two girls were like peas in a pod, as close as sisters could ever be—which meant that most times Lori dressed and behaved older than her years, while every now and then Dana seemed like a teenager again.

"It's Lebna," Dana replied.

"Ah, pretty boy, have you heard from him?"

She shook her head. "Nothing. I'm going round to his place, see if he's there."

"I've told your sister she should let one of my guys go round there first, just to be on the safe side," Danjuma said. "Or at least let one of them go with her. But you know what she's like, stubborn as an ox."

"Easily solved, let's go together," Lori offered.

Silent glances were exchanged between the three of them. The problem was that Danjuma could hardly object. They were in no danger as long as they were in the town; no one would dare to so much as speak to them. Everyone knew who the girls were, and who their father was, which was both a blessing and curse.

"It's early yet," said Danjuma, checking his watch.

"Doesn't matter," Lori said. "If we go now, we're more likely to catch him if he's screwing around behind Dana's back."

"Lori!" Danjuma and Dana said in unison, but the girl just gave them a defiant look.

"Well, it's true, isn't it? Admit it, that's what you're both thinking."

It certainly was what Danjuma was thinking.

There was no danger of any surprises waiting for them inside the apartment, except for Lebna's naked ass bumping uglies with some whore. That would hurt her, and he hated the idea of Dana in pain. He would kill the boy with his bare hands if he broke her heart.

He thought about it, mind on fire.

If he was quick, he might be able to get someone round there before his girls got there. They still had to get ready, and with that pair, it could take an hour to make themselves presentable. Or it could take thirty seconds.

Was an hour enough to scour the place, find out where he'd gone, and remove anything that might lead the girls there?

Maybe.

Maybe not.

Danjuma waited until they'd left the room before he stepped outside and made the call.

Before he'd finished his second cup of coffee, both daughters were ready to leave.

"That was quick," he said.

"Well, if he is a scumbag, we want to catch him at it, not give him room to wriggle out of it," Lori said, flatly, and with the kind of dispassionate reasoning that had Danjuma wondering where her childhood had gone.

"But you've not had breakfast yet," he said, but they weren't going to be slowed.

The moment they left the house he called the man again.

"Rakeem," he said. "Where are you?"

"On my way to the boy's place."

"How long is it going to take you to get there?"

"Twenty minutes."

"Too long," Danjuma said. He'd never get there, search and clear the room, even if that meant throwing out some naked woman sucking off that stupid boy and get out of there before the girls arrived. He was just going to have to trust that Lebna wasn't an idiot. "Leave it. I'll talk to you later."

He hung up without waiting for a response.

CHAPTER
SEVEN

Connors woke to the pounding of someone taking a jackhammer to his skull and a sour taste in his mouth.

Even without opening his eyes he could see the sunlight creeping in around the edges of the heavy blackout curtains. Those curtains were the closest thing to a touch of luxury in the room.

It took him a moment to remember where he was, and another to recall what had happened the night before.

He remembered Travis and the whisky but not a great deal else.

Then he half-remembered collapsing back on the bed, still clutching the bag of drugs they'd bought from Danjuma and only then did he finally open his eyes.

The pain increased tenfold, but so did the sense of panic.

He reached across the bed, fumbling around in search of the attaché case, feeling nothing but empty mattress.

Hating himself, he sat. A wave of nausea overwhelmed him. He swallowed back the bile.

"Where the fuck is it?" he said.

There was no answer.

Looking down at his gut and his shriveled cock he rocked slightly forward; it wasn't a pretty sight. He sucked it in and pulled his flaccid prick away from where it stuck to his pasty white thigh and blew out a heavy sigh.

"Where's the fucking case?" He asked the bundle of quilt on the sofa. Partly shrouded in shadow, it didn't move.

"Travis! Wake up you little cunt, what the fuck have you done with the case?"

Still no reply.

He could make out the shape of his boxers at the foot of the bed, along with the pile of jeans he'd obviously wriggled out of. He reached for them, having to slow as he leaned forward, the threat of vomit making itself known. He made a grab for them but had to pause and catch a breath before he puked. He pulled the jeans on, then swung his legs around. His shoes were on the carpet. He reached down for one, then hurled it in the direction of the sofa.

He hit the bundle of comforter and blankets but got no response as the shape of the man beneath deflated.

He was hit by the realization that had him cursing for a full sixty seconds as he got unsteadily to his feet and stumbled across the room. Connors pulled the comforter aside. Travis had gone. He'd bulked up pillows to pretend to be his shape. Right then, that second, Connors would have preferred to see a corpse lying there.

It took no time to check the rest of the room, and he sobered up pretty fucking fast. Travis was gone, the case along with him.

He went to the bathroom, no longer able to hold it back, and puked his guts up. There was a moment as the shit came out of him that he feared it would never stop.

He rinsed his face in cold water then looked at his ashen reflection in the mirror.

"Fuck."

It was the only word he seemed able to get out of his mouth.

It didn't even begin to come close to expressing how he felt.

Travis had fucked him.

The cunt was gone, the cocaine and the hire car, too.

And then an even bigger panic sank in. He rushed across the room to his own suitcase, tossing items aside with increasing desperation, even as he knew he'd been right, the bastard had taken his passport too.

He was beyond fucked.

He was in a hell with no way of getting home.

Not that he could face going home with the money men waiting for him, and their slice. And right then, he figured maybe he was better off staying here, begging Danjuma for work. "Fuck," he said again. Sol Danjuma was the only person he'd met here who had any influence. But what was it going to cost him to ask for help?

In the haze of the hangover, and the ever-increasing headache, Connors decided that Danjuma was the answer to his prayers, however fucked up those prayers might be—although admittedly right now they didn't go much beyond tracking down Travis and executing the motherfucker.

His phone was still on the nightstand.

Travis hadn't taken it.

He made the call.

It was answered on the third ring.

"Who the fuck is this?" came the voice.

"It's Connors," he said, though he was pretty sure that his name would have appeared on the screen of the other man's phone, unless he'd deleted his contact details already.

"Connor's? Am I supposed to recognize that name? Are you somebody I should know?" A sharp sniff. "Doesn't mean anything to me. What do you want?"

"The drugs you sold me yesterday," he started.

"Ah, the American. I hope you're not going to try to say there's something wrong with our arrangement? I know my merchandise is pure."

"No, no, nothing like that."

"Then what, Mr. American? You want to buy some more already?"

Connors took a deep breath. "It's been stolen," he blurted it out in a rush, sooner than he'd intended to. He knew there was fear in his voice.

The roar of laughter at the other end of the phone wasn't what he'd been hoping to hear.

"And just what the fuck do you expect *me* to do about that?" Danjuma said, then suddenly his tone changed. "Or are you trying to insinuate that this unfortunate series of events has something to do with me?"

"No, no, not at all. Nothing like that," Connors said in a rush to placate the drug kingpin. "I know exactly who's taken it."

"It was that partner of yours, wasn't it?" There was a moment, a beat, gloating. "I knew he was the smart one."

"He wasn't my partner. He worked for me."

"Then more fool you," he said. "It's one thing to be ripped off by a partner, another to be robbed by the hired help."

"There's more."

"More? What more can there be?"

"He's taken my passport."

"It is not your day, is it, Mr. American? How did you let this happen? Was there a woman involved? She fuck your brains out? There's usually a woman. No, don't tell me, you sampled the merchandise, didn't you? You are a weak man."

"No, nothing like that," Connors protested, but Danjuma was right, he was a weak man. "We had a few drinks last night. I didn't drink that much, but this morning I woke up with the hangover from hell."

"So, he drugged your drink," Danjuma said. "You are not a very clever man, are you, Mr. American? Still there is not a lot you can do about it now."

"Can you help me?"

"Me? Why should I?"

"Because I've got no one else to turn to. I can't even afford to eat. I'll die out here."

"That is not my problem. If you had money, then maybe."

Conners tried to work out how much he could scrape together. "I can get some… I think… make a call, have it wired here."

"Then perhaps you can afford to hire my help for a few hours. How long ago do you think your friend left?"

"He's no friend of mine," Connors corrected. Danjuma was fucking with him. He shouldn't rise to the bait. "A few hours, maybe."

"Or he could have been gone half the night."

"I suppose."

"So, tell me, how were you intending to get the merchandise out of the country?" Danjuma asked. "It is safe to assume he will use the same route as everything is already in place."

It made sense. "We were taking it to the coast and meeting a yacht."

"And sailing back to America on this yacht?"

"No, it belongs to one of the partners in the syndicate."

"Another partner? A syndicate? It sounds as though you have been stretching the truth a little thin, Mr. American. I thought you were the main man? I didn't realize you were working for others."

"Does it matter how many of us were involved?"

"Not to me it doesn't. You're the one taking the risks. But tell me, what is stopping this yacht guy from disappearing with your merchandise? You have a lot of weak links in your chain."

"Well, he's not one of them. He has too much to lose."

"Maybe. So how were you getting back home?"

"Flying. We wouldn't be carrying anything with us so there would be nothing stopping us."

"And the tickets?"

Connors didn't answer.

He didn't need to.

Another laugh. "He's taken those, too, hasn't he?"

They both knew the answer.

"Stay where you are," Danjuma said. "One of my men will come and get you."

"'How do you know where I am?"

I know everything that happens in this town. I own it."

CHAPTER
EIGHT

Daudi was glad that his friend had decided to come with him.

He'd been prepared to do it on his own. Hell, part of him still thought it would be better if he did. If this fucked up, then he'd be the only one facing Boss's temper. He would accept whatever punishment was meted out. But, having someone with him meant that it was twice as likely to succeed and only half as likely to fail.

Daudi was driving.

It was one of the beat-up old junkers they kept in the compound for runs into Freetown.

This one was an old Trabant, a long way from home. It was big and clunky and would do a lot of damage if it ran into anything... or anyone.

There was little but dust between the compound and Freetown, miles and miles of barren wasteland. Desolation. It was a no man's land, unwanted and unloved.

The town itself was full of life though.

Most of the local bars were more than happy to take their money, not the least because they paid in US Dollars, which was so much more than the local currency. The same could be said for the girls who offered themselves up for cold hard cash. There had been a girl, once upon a time, that Daudi had visited a few times. He liked to think that he'd been falling in love with her, like it was a normal relationship, but she didn't do feelings. It didn't matter to her who knocked on her door as long as they had dollars in their pockets and were gone thirty minutes later. Still, he could think of her on those lonely nights in his bunk. Now, he wasn't even sure that he could remember her name. Her breasts, though, those he would never forget.

"How many laundromats do you think there can be?" Musa said. "We could be driving around for hours looking."

"We could, but there are only four," Daudi said, smiling.

"I have done my research. Trust me. Four."

"That is not so many."

"No, it isn't. And how many will have an apartment above them?"

"If we find the right one, what then?"

"We get inside. If we are lucky, we will find something that will tell us who the mystery woman is. That would be a start."

Daudi slowed the Trabant as they reached the outskirts of Freetown.

He didn't want to draw attention to them by driving too fast, but he wanted to be there now. He felt it in his bones, trouble brewing. This was strictly in and out as quickly as possible.

He pulled over to the side of the road. He had marked the first of the laundromats on a paper map. He'd thought about using the

GPS function on his phone, but had no idea if Boss monitored that sort of thing. He'd grown up in a township where the governor was the only person who had a phone of their own, though there was a payphone in the general store the township shared. He instinctively didn't trust technology because it still felt alien to him, deep in his core.

The first address turned out to be a single-story affair; a purpose-built place constructed from cinder block and concrete render.

It wasn't what they were looking for.

The second on the map was more promising, but the woman running the washers beneath it was adamant that there was no apartment upstairs, just a storeroom where they kept their chemicals. That might or might not have been true, but while they were there a middle-aged man came in, told the woman he had an appointment upstairs, and she let him through, meaning something was going on up there beyond storage. It didn't take long to figure out what, as a regular line of men of a certain age turned up. She was running a brothel up there. Wrong place again. Two down, two to go.

"We could stay, check the girls out."

"You'll need an appointment," the woman said. "Our girls are very good, very beautiful, which means they are very busy. Time is money. Make an appointment."

"We might just do that," Musa said, as Daudi steered him towards the door.

They hit lucky with the third. "Yes," the owner said. "I know Lebna, he's nice man. Very clean and pays his rent on time, but I haven't seen him in a few days. Are you friends of his?"

"We are," Daudi said. "He's been asking us to visit and meet this young lady of his. I don't suppose you know where we might find her?"

And then, just like that, her expression changed. It was as though she'd realized she shouldn't be talking to them. That just made Daudi all the more curious about the girl. Who the fuck was she?

"When he turns up, I'll tell him to give you a call, shall I?"

"You do that," Daudi, said. "Tell him Daudi called around."

"Of course," the woman promised.

As they turned to leave there was the sound of footsteps above them.

"Maybe that's him," she said. "There's a side door outside. Why don't you just go up and surprise him?"

CHAPTER
NINE

"He's not here," Lori said as she stepped inside.

"You sound disappointed."

"What can I say? If he's screwing around, I want to catch him screwing around," she laughed. "Then maybe you'll finally get him out of that pretty little head of yours, sis."

"Hah! Well, *I'm* glad he's not here." She blew out her cheeks. "But that doesn't help much. I still want to know what's happened to him"

"Something so bad he can't call you, or text. Get real, sis. He's just like all the others."

Dana knew that her little sister was right—or at least probably right—and that Lebna was with another woman, but she couldn't bring herself to believe it. He had said he loved her. Not that he was the first boy to say those words. Every single one of them did, every time they wanted to peel down her panties.

But she had believed him when he said it.

She'd never doubted him when he said that he wanted to be with her forever. She heard only the truth when he said he wanted to share a home together. And she said yes when he wanted to marry her. But then, there had been others who had said that, too, but she hadn't said yes to them. They'd been looking for a way to worm their way into her family, get close to her father. Lebna didn't even know who he was, let alone what he did in this town.

"I'll check the bedroom, shall I?" Lori offered.

"No," Dana had to do that for herself.

That was their place.

It was where they were at their most intimate. She didn't want her sister intruding on that space.

"You check the bathroom."

The bed had not been made, but that was not unusual.

She doubted Lebna had ever made a bed in his life.

He'd promised that he would change.

Maybe he would, but it was never going to be easy to break the habits of a lifetime. He was who he was because of the way he had grown up. The truth was that she loved him for it not despite it.

She checked the sheets, afraid of what she might find.

They were clean and for Lebna reasonably fresh.

There hadn't been another woman in this bed since she had last been here.

His clothes were still in the closet and his shoes on the floor, one upright the other tipped on its side as if they had been kicked off as he sat on the bed. She could just picture him doing it.

"Nothing in there," said Lori. Standing in the doorway. "You see anything in here?"

Dana shook her head, then spotted the photograph of her that he kept at the side of the bed.

She picked it up, convinced now that whatever had happened to him, he wasn't cheating on her. He would not have left this out.

"Nothing," she said then put it carefully back in place.

There was no hint of where he'd gone or when he would be coming back. "Maybe he said something to the woman downstairs?" she suggested, as she started to leave the room.

Dana took one last lingering look around the bedroom she'd shared with the love of her life and returned to the living room. It looked like he could have walked out five minutes ago and be back at any time.

"Maybe I should just wait here?" she said. "He has to come back sooner or later."

"Does he?" Her sister asked. She ignored the inference. She had never felt like this before, not for any man. She'd always been the one to give them the cold shoulder, ghosting them until they got the message.

But here she was, prepared to sit around waiting for someone when she had no idea of when he would return.

Or if.

"Is this his phone?"

Lori picked something up from the floor.

Dana took it from her.

It explained why he hadn't been answering her calls, and why he hadn't let her know where he had gone. What it didn't explain was what it was doing on the floor, half-kicked under the couch.

It didn't feel good.

Dana was still wondering what the absolute worst it might mean, when she heard footsteps on the stairwell outside and felt the sudden kickstart of her heart rate.

"He's here!" she said. "You don't need to hang around."

"You mean make yourself scarce, sis, because I need to jump his bones."

"It's like you read my mind," she said.

Then she heard voices on the stairs and knew that neither of them belonged to the man she'd come to find.

CHAPTER
TEN

Danjuma tried to set aside the seething anger he felt at the American's temerity. How did he have the gall to call and beg for his help? In Sol Danjuma's world you got yourself off the shit or you drowned in it.

But he could wait.

Danjuma would get someone to go and pick him up, later, after he had sweated and panicked and learned his place in the food chain. He sure as hell wasn't going to do anything about the American just because the man had begged. No, it had to be on his terms, advantageous to him. That way it became good business, not charity.

For now, he had someone waiting for him; someone who deserved his undivided attention.

"Everything okay, my love?" Dominique asked when he returned to the bedroom.

He had only stepped out to get another bottle of wine from the cooler when the phone had rung.

The woman was something special.

Without doubt, the most beautiful woman he had ever spent time with, and yet she expected little from him.

She didn't want to be his wife along with all the trappings that might have meant, nor was she interested in looking elsewhere for those benefits.

He couldn't be sure that it would always be this way, but for now she would give him anything he asked for, do anything he wanted, without question and without complaint, and he would do the same for her in return, no questions asked.

And yet it wasn't love.

She was strong, athletic as well as beautiful, and with that edge to her personality that assured she would be dangerous if crossed. She could probably hold her own in a clean fight with most of his men. Just the way he liked it.

"Just business," he said and topped up her glass, unable to take his eyes from the sheen of sweat on her breasts that had almost dried. It would leave her skin salty. He had the sudden urge to lick it off her. The thought of it was enough to make him hard again, but there was no rush. He intended to savor her.

"I need to be going soon," she said, putting down her glass. She checked her phone on the nightstand, lying down on her side, facing away from him.

"How soon?" He asked, putting down his own glass.

He settled down to be close to her, pressing as much of his skin against hers as he could, before kissing her back softly, tracing one of the scars that marked her skin.

He knew that she had been Special Forces, but she refused to say when or for which country.

That was all in the past.

The past did not matter, she insisted when he had tried to tease the information out of her.

She pushed herself closer, pressing her cheeks against his erection and moving slowly in a steady rhythm.

"Not too soon," she assured him.

She leaned away from Danjuma, peeling skin from skin, and offering herself to him; an offer he could not resist.

He slipped inside her, still slick and ready for him.

"I'm glad," he said, falling in time with her movements, one hand on the curve of her hip to keep her close as he slipped in and out, in long, slow strokes. He slid his hand around her and eased it between her legs, pressing to increase her pleasure. She placed her own hand on top of his, guiding him and becoming insistent. Demanding.

"Don't stop," she husked.

He had no intention of stopping, but he knew it would not be long before the urgency began to build, and he'd have no choice but to surrender to it.

She moved her hand, raising it to the pillow, and clasped her other hand as her back arched, pushing against him harder, faster.

She was moments away from climax and he knew it.

He had seen the signs often enough.

He pushed against her, skin slapping against skin.

When she came, he allowed himself his own release.

Danjuma stayed close, not willing to pull away.

He kissed her shoulder again, and this time all she gave was a contended purr.

CHAPTER
ELEVEN

Daudi paused as he reached the top of the stairs.

He raised a finger to his lips, indicating silence.

The door was ajar meaning whoever they had heard from the laundromat still likely in there.

Part of him wished he'd brought a gun, even if that escalated things fast. There was one in the glove compartment of the Trabant. He contemplated sending Musa back to get it.

Slowly, he pushed the door open, just a fraction wider, so that he could see into a lounge area.

The place was silent.

He couldn't see anyone.

He took a step inside. The room was both a living, dining and kitchenette space all in one. It was a long way from luxury, but it was clean.

It made sense that the door on the opposite wall led to the bathroom and bedroom. There wasn't space up here for more than one. He motioned for Musa to follow him and headed for the door. He paused for a moment, listening for sounds of life on the other side.

Still nothing, only silence.

There was every chance whoever was on the other side of the door was holding a weapon, aimed squarely at the middle of the door, ready to pump their guts full of lead.

He could feel his heartbeat in his throat.

He didn't want to move. Moving broke the moment. Moving got someone dead.

A second later he heard the clatter of footsteps on metal.

"The fire escape!" He barked. "Get out there, stop them." Musa didn't need telling twice. Daudi charged through the door. No bullets punched into his gut. The door led to two more.

He threw the first open. The bathroom. Empty.

He tried the other.

It didn't budge. Something was blocking it from the other side.

He pushed at it, putting his shoulder into it and straining until he finally felt it begin to move, barely, wood scraping against wood. His shoes slipped across the floor as he scrabbled for more purchase, but eventually he'd shoved whatever piece of furniture had been wedged up against the door out of the way enough to squeeze into the room.

The window was open. There was barely enough breeze to ruffle the curtains.

He stuck his head out, seeing the fire escape, and on the ground below, Musa struggling with a girl who was trying her hardest to wriggle free. He had a tight grip on her. She was going nowhere. The problem was the moment she realized that she started shouting loud enough to draw attention.

Musa slapped a hand across her mouth.

She tried to bite it.

Daudi hurried down as people started to emerge from doorways and heads looked out from opened windows.

They didn't need the attention.

And they absolutely didn't need to be remembered.

"Get her in the fucking car," he said without thinking.

They needed to get out of there fast, and that meant a choice of leaving the girl behind or taking her with them. Leave her, they lost her forever, and with her the chance of finding out who had killed Lebna.

He held the rear door open as Musa bundled the girl inside.

She was feisty.

Musa took a couple of nasty kicks that would leave him with a nice falsetto for a while.

"Get in the back with her," Daudi told him, ignoring his pain.

He clambered in the front and started the engine, putting his foot on the gas. The Trabant peeled away from the curbside, leaving a cloud of dust behind as they sped away. Without taking his eyes off the road, Daudi reached across and flipped the glove compartment open, retrieving the desert eagle from inside with one hand.

"Shut the fuck up!" He snarled at the girl. "One more fucking sound and I'll put a fucking bullet in your head. You feel me?"

"Fuck you! You wouldn't dare," she spat back.

"Maybe not," he said. "But fucking up your knees wouldn't kill you. And that I very much would dare."

That was enough to at least stop her struggling. For a moment. "My father isn't going to like this. You know that don't you? He'll want to hurt you for this," she said.

"We just want to talk to you," Daudi said.

"Do you kidnap everyone you *just* want to talk to?"

She slumped into the seat and folded her arms.

At least she didn't look like she was about to do something stupid like throw herself out of the moving car.

"Only the mouthy ones who kick me in the *cajones*," Musa gruffed.

The girl didn't even try to hide the smile. "My father taught me never to talk to strange men."

"She's got you there," Daudi said. And damned, but he was starting to like the girl. She was maybe sixteen, with a face full of makeup, so probably considerably younger.

It didn't make sense that Lebna would lose his mind for a kid.

"So where are you taking me for this little heart-to-heart?"

"You'll know soon enough," Daudi said.

Musa said nothing.

Daudi had been tempted to just ask the questions, find out what she knew, then dump her at the roadside. But he couldn't shake the fear he'd forget to ask something crucial and be on the wrong end of Boss' wrath.

Better to just deliver the girl and let him do the questioning.

He adjusted the mirror to catch sight of Musa.

He nodded when they made eye contact.

He understood and agreed.

CHAPTER
TWELVE

Dana started running the moment her feet hit the ground.

Her too-high heels made it difficult, but she wasn't about to slow down.

Instead, she paused barely long enough to kick them up and snatch them, then ran as if her life depended on it.

Pushing the closet against the door had been a good idea, even if it had taken a few seconds, it had bought them a lot more time to get out of there. Lori was only a few yards behind her.

"Just keep running," Dana yelled back over her shoulder.

Her little car was parked over the road, but halfway down the fire escape she realized she'd left her purse inside the apartment, along with her keys in it. And her phone.

First priority, get away, far away, then come back later, when whoever these men were had gone.

She reached a doorway and paused long enough for Lori to catch up, but there was no sign of her.

Her stomach dropped as she heard her sister call out.

She stepped out of the doorway, ready to run back and help, even as other people came to see what the shouting was, and panicked at the sight of her little sister being bundled into a battered old car. Before she could do anything, its engine burst into life, shaking free rust and belching smoke out of its tailpipe, before it took off in a cloud of dust.

She fumbled for her phone, and nearly dropped it as her body refused to obey her, not even thinking about who she was calling. It was all instinct. Her fingers trembled across the screen. A voice answered a moment later.

"Dad," she said, but then lost the words to a rush of tears and sobs that choked her up.

Her knees buckled and she sagged back against the building, her back sliding slowly down the wall.

She could hear her father's voice through the tiny speaker, but she couldn't find the words to answer him.

She had no idea what had happened—or why—only that it was her fault. And her sister was in trouble.

A gentle hand helped Dana to her feet and led her inside.

At some point someone took her phone from her and spoke to her father on her behalf, explaining, taking control.

She wasn't the one breaking the news to him.

She couldn't.

Eventually, she recognized the middle-aged woman fussing around her, constantly asking if she needed anything and reassuring her that her father would be there soon.

Mama Sula had run her little café for as long as Dana could remember. She took no nonsense from anyone and was more than happy to turf out anyone who disrespected her, without fear of any reaction or reprisal.

Dana always liked this place, with its clean, crisp white tablecloths unlike the battered Formica topped tables that most places had.

There were only a few customers sitting at tables that morning. Dana didn't' care. She was only vaguely aware of the eyes that kept glancing in her direction. Maybe they knew what had happened in the street, maybe they even knew who she was. She didn't care. And their gossip was kept to whispers so she was spared it.

She was still feeling lost and confused when the café door opened.

The place fell utterly silent.

"Dana," the familiar voice said, and then her father had lifted her and wrapped his arms around her and for a moment it felt like all the pain in the world would go away. She leaned towards him, and the tears came again, though this time there was relief in them. He was here. He would make everything alright. That was what he did. He took care of everything.

When Sol Danjuma eventually released her, he pulled out a chair and sat with his hands still holding hers, not ready to break the contact.

"Tell me what happened," he said. "Everything you can remember."

The story came out in fits and starts, none of it told in the right order, but that didn't matter. Danjuma remained patient, listening, absorbing, thinking. Dana knew that he had to be worried for her sister, every bit as much as she was, but he didn't show it. He protected an aura of calm power. There was no anger, no impatience.

"Give me a moment, dear heart. I will be right back," he said and smiled at Mama Sula.

"Perhaps some sweet tea, dear?" The older woman said as Dana's father opened the door back out into the street.

He would find Lori.

He had to.

But she couldn't understand why anyone would take her little sister... or why they would even *dare*.

Dana knew what her father was, and what he was capable of, even though he did his best to hide it.

It was as if he lived two separate lives, or maybe three.

Dana knew about the woman he went to see in town some nights, too, but as her mother was no longer with them, she could hardly complain about him finding comfort in some other woman's arms. He was always happier after he had seen her, and life was better when he was happy. Dana didn't even know the woman's name, and she was happy enough for it to stay that way.

She watched him through the glass. He was deep in conversation with one of his men, but she couldn't tell who it was.

He would already have people looking for her sister.

He would have her back home before she knew it.

Dana was still trying to convince herself that when he came back inside.

"Let's go," he told her, and took her by the wrist. He wasn't hurting her; his grip was firm but not too tight. He wasn't about to let go of her.

"Where are we going?" she asked. "Do you know who took her? Do you know where she is?"

"Not here," he said. "Home."

CHAPTER
THIRTEEN

"What the fuck are we doin'?" Musa asked.

Daudi glanced in the rearview mirror and saw Musa struggling to keep the girl in her seat. She seemed determined to throw herself into traffic. She'd already tried to claw his eyes out and scramble into the front like some possessed wild cat. Right now, Musa was getting the worst of her claws.

"We're taking her somewhere quiet. We need to know what she knows," Daudi repeated. He'd said it half a dozen times since they'd snatched her off the street. It wasn't sinking in. He kept trying to see if there was anyone following them, but the only thing back there was dust.

The buildings had long since thinned out.

Give it a few more minutes and they'd be on the outskirts of Freetown.

If all they needed was quiet, anywhere here would do. But on some subconscious level, another part of him was steering them back towards the compound. Let Boss decide what to do with her. Let Boss ask the questions.

It would be better that way.

"I ain't telling you shit," the girl snapped. "And when my father finds you two fucking creeps are gonna wish you'd never been born."

"I wish that every day," Daudi said.

Musa laughed. "We ain't afraid of yo daddy, little girl. Whoever the fuck he is, he needs to know his place. Now, you gonna tell us everything you know and then we'll let you go. Nice and simple. No one needs to get hurt. But if you don't, well then things are gonna be bad for you. There's some really bad men where we're going, an' some of them ain't seen a woman in *months*, if you know what I mean, little thing?"

"Fuck you."

He gave a sudden grunt of pain.

Daudi knew that she'd found a soft target.

A moment later she turned her attention to him.

He swerved the car hard, slamming on the brakes.

She almost came flying into the front seat, but it was enough to take the wind out of her.

Musa pulled her back into the seat.

Daudi heard a slap of hand on cheek, harder than maybe needed. Daudi hit the accelerator again, giving another glance over his shoulder. The girl was cowering now, and suddenly looking very young. Much younger than he had thought. She was vulnerable and he felt like shit.

For the first time, he was wondering if they'd fucked up.

He'd figured she was the girlfriend, that she'd lured Lebna into town and in the end had him done for, but not anymore. That nagging doubt that she looked older than she really was, had solidified into certainty. She was far too young. Lebna was a lot of things, but he was no pedo.

What the fuck had they done?

He slowed down a little once they had finally left the last of the buildings behind. There was still a way to go, but the quality of the road quickly deteriorated, and the car rocked and juddered as they went. If he'd kept up the speed they'd been traveling at, the suspension wouldn't have held up to the battering. He slowed, which meant they were kicking up less dust. Now, at least, he could see behind them.

There was no sign of a tail.

Before long he could make out the shape of the compound in the distance.

"You fuckers are going to be in for some real shit when my father finds out what you've done," the girl fronted. She'd recovered enough of herself to face them down, bravado in her words even if her voice didn't carry the same level of confidence.

Daudi said nothing.

He concentrated on the road, practicing in his head what he was going to say to Boss when they presented him with the girl.

He was way past having doubts.

They shouldn't have brought her here. They should have driven back into Freetown and ditched her at the side of the road. But she'd seen their faces well enough to cause problems if her father really was someone like she seemed to think.

Everything was spiraling out of control.

"You just keep your mouth shut, bitch," Musa snarled, "unless you want another slap."

"Leave her alone," Daudi said. "She's just a kid," Daudi said.

"Yeah, a kid who dick-punched me."

Daudi tried not to let a smile play across his lips, but it wasn't easy.

Ahead of them, the gates of the compound loomed large. He slowed even more until the rusty old Trabant finally came to a stop.

Someone keeping watch up on the wall waved a hand. He couldn't see who from this angle. They shouted down to someone below them. Less than a minute later the gates were swinging open, grating across the hard-packed dirt road, to let them through.

Daudi should have felt relief, but instead there was a kind of dread building, tying his guts in knots.

It didn't help that Boss was waiting for them in the courtyard and he didn't look happy.

"Where the *fuck* have you two been?" Boss demanded the moment that Daudi stepped out of the car.

"Town," he answered.

"And what the fuck were you doing there?"

"I didn't think..."

"And that's always the fucking problem with you. You *never* think. And why the fuck is that idiot just sitting there clutching his prick?"

Musa clambered out slowly but didn't say a word in his own defense.

Daudi was relieved. Whatever he'd said would have only made matters worse. He was about to tell Boss about the girl when the other passenger door opened, and she stepped out.

"And who the fuck is this?" There was no doubting the anger in his voice.

"My name is Lori Danjuma," the girl said defiantly, arms folded in front of her. "Now, my turn to ask a question. Who the fuck are *you?*"

CHAPTER
FOURTEEN

Connors paced his room. He couldn't keep his eyes off the clock.

His bags were packed. He was ready to leave. There was nothing to keep him in this shithole a minute longer than he had to be here. There was also the little problem of not being able to pay for the room, even if he got cash wired back from the States. Especially if Danjuma expected him to stump up cash to pay for his help.

He'd already been waiting close to two hours. It was hard not to think that Danjuma was jerking his chain.

The temptation was to call him again, but what would that gain him? Danjuma would either send one of his men, or he wouldn't. He was trying to make a list of anyone else he could call, but right now it was a list with no names on it.

There was a knock on his door.

He abandoned his pacing to open it.

A big man stood on the other side, filling the space that the door had vacated.

"Time to go," the big man said.

Connors paused for a moment, suddenly unsure if he was doing the right thing. The big man turned and started to walk away, not bothered if Connors was following him or not. People did what he told them to.

Connors grabbed his things and hurried down the corridor after him.

For a giant, the man moved with surprising pace.

Connors had to hurry to catch up with him.

"Where are we going?" he asked as he ducked to get into the jeep parked in the hotel lot. It was an off-roader. The bodywork was splashed and spattered with mud.

"Does it matter?"

"Guess not," Connors admitted. There was nothing for him here and no one else he could put his trust in. If Danjuma had sent this man to take care of him at least it would all be over soon enough, one way or another.

He had the engine running before Connors had buckled up.

A moment later the car lurched and swung through the tightest U-turn Connors had ever experienced, the g-forces slamming him up against the door as he struggled with the seatbelt. He'd managed to secure it just as the driver slammed on the brakes at an intersection.

They hurtled through the streets for the next ten minutes. For most of them, Connors was in fear of his life.

"How badly have you fucked up?" the man asked eventually.

"What has Danjuma told you?"

"He ain't told me anything. He didn't need to."

"Then how…?"

"When people deal with Danjuma they tend to get their asses out of here with their merchandise as soon as they can. They don't call asking favors. So, stands to reason, you fucked up."

"I was robbed," Connors said.

"Tell me you ain't dumb enough to think *we* did it?" The man took his eyes from the road to glare him down. He showed no signs of slowing.

"No," Connors said. "I know exactly who stole it."

"Ah, no honor amongst cunts, eh? You been fucked over by your partner," the man laughed, his mouth so wide that it seemed to split his face. It was as if he was transformed into a completely different person. "Nice." And in that moment the threatening hulk had been replaced by something far less sinister. It was strange how being ridiculed made him feel more at ease.

Instead of being taken to the same place where he had met Danjuma the night before, the jeep came to a halt outside an imposing house set behind a high wall. He saw razor wire on the top.

"Is this Danjuma's house?" Connors asked, realizing it was a stupid question the moment the words left his lips. The big man grunted, and the sour expression returned to his face. He wound down his window and reached out to press a button on an intercom.

A moment later a pair of imposing doors swung open and allowed them inside.

The driveway was short, but it was enough to ensure Connors saw the two armed men standing guard outside the front door.

His first instinct was: *who was Danjuma trying to keep out*, but the second was maybe more telling, *or who is he trying to keep in?* Because he didn't need this level of security just to protect wealth. No one would be foolish enough to raid the place, not even the police. The man controlled a small army in his operation, with the same kind of firepower.

One of the guards approached as the jeep came to a halt.

"Stay here," the big man said.

The driver's side window was still open. Neither man made any effort to keep their voices down. Whatever they had to say to each other wasn't secret. That should have been a relief to Connors. If they'd brought him here to kill him, he doubted they'd talk openly about it. It didn't take long to figure out they were talking about Danjuma.

"He's not been back long," the guard said. "He had his eldest with him."

"What about Lori?"

The guard shook his head. "I have not been told where she is," he said.

"But there have been whispers."

The guard looked around but said nothing.

"I'd rather know what I'm walking into in there."

"They say she's been kidnapped."

A beat. Silence. Then, "By who?"

The guard shook his head, but this time because he genuinely didn't know, not because he was reluctant to share. "He says he wants to see you as soon as you got here."

The big man nodded. "And I'm guessing it's not about him." He jerked his head in the direction of the jeep.

Connors was starting to get the feeling that there was something far bigger than his fuck up going on here.

He didn't know if that was good or bad for him.

CHAPTER
FIFTEEN

"Tell me again," said Danjuma. "This time, everything, from the beginning."

"I told you," Dana said. "We spoke to the woman who runs the shop..."

"From the beginning," He snapped. "Who is the boy? Where does he come from? Who are his friends? I need to know all of it."

"What has that got to do with anything?" she asked.

Danjuma shook his head and released a sigh of exasperation. "It's got everything to do with everything, child. If he wasn't one of them, then he might know who they are. It could even have been him they were looking for, not your sister."

"Then why take Lori? That doesn't make any sense."

"On the contrary, it makes absolute sense. They are looking for him and think that she might be able to help them find him, see? The problem is they don't know who she is, only that they found her in his apartment. The alternative is they know who she is, and they took her to get at me. But let's not go there yet."

He watched her face and waited.

Shouting at her wasn't going to get him anywhere, no matter how angry or frightened he was. He needed to be calm. Sooner or later there would be tears. If he was going to get anything out of her, he needed to give her time.

"Do you think they'll hurt her?"

She was starting to put the pieces together in her head.

"They might," he said. "If they think she knows something she isn't telling them."

"But she doesn't know *anything*."

"But you do, so tell me what you know about this boy." Danjuma was already cursing himself for not doing his due diligence on the boy. But right now all that mattered was bringing Lori home safely. Recriminations could come later.

Dana started to tell him what she knew about Lebna.

He'd heard that damned name often enough, and already knew they had met at the nightclub, but not much more than that. His excuse was that he'd been too busy, but the truth was he'd been negligent. He should have made an effort to know more when it came to the safety of his children.

"He came over the border maybe a year ago, after his parents were killed. A few of them came together. He said they all looked out for each other, but that now we had met he wanted us to have a life together."

"Does he have a job?"

"He wouldn't talk about it," she said.

"He thought it would be better if you didn't know?" Danjuma had said the same words to Dana's mother many times. It was better if she didn't know. That way she couldn't tell anyone anything.

"But he's not part of that anymore. That was why we got the apartment."

The final pieces of the puzzle dropped into place for him, but all she did was shrug. She knew exactly what the boy was doing, just as Danjuma's wife had all those years ago.

"These friends," he tried instead, "Have you met any of them? Do you know where they live?" They weren't 'friends' at all. They weren't refugees, either. They were a displaced cartel that had moved into his territory, the kind of organization that looked out for each other, but was impossible to leave. He knew who they were without knowing exactly who they were. How could he not? They had been making inroads into his territory of late. Those inroads came at a price. So, was this about him after all? Had they taken his little girl to hurt him? He would never forgive himself if that was the case. Danjuma had made a mistake here. He'd been worried the boy was an opportunist looking to snake his way up this particular drainpipe, to get to Danjuma through his girls.

He hadn't realized just how wrong he'd got it though.

She shook her head again and this time he could see that the tears were not far away. "They live out of town somewhere. That's all I know."

He was one of them, living out in the compound outside of Freetown. That made sense. Those bastards had caused him nothing but grief since they'd rocked up a year ago. He should have come down on them with wrath and furious vengeance and just crushed them instead of thinking live and let live. Well, he would take a fucking war to their gates if he had to.

"What about the car? Had you seen it before?"

This time she paused before answering. "Maybe," she said. "When we used to meet up, before he moved into town, he used to drive different cars. They were all old and beat up, like this one. What does that mean, Daddy?"

"It means that the men who took your sister were friends of his."

"But why would they take Lori?"

"I don't know, but I will find out, I promise you that."

For now, he had no intention of telling her about the boy about his so-called friends and just how stupid she'd been bringing this shit to their door.

Instead, he reached an arm around her and pulled her tight, letting her sob into his chest.

CHAPTER
SIXTEEN

Boss looked at the girl. What the fuck did they think they were doing by bringing her here?

"Danjuma?" he said, recognizing the name.

She nodded. "And when my father finds out what you've done, you're lives are not going to be worth living."

Boss chuckled, enjoying her braggadocio. The girl had spirit, that was for sure, and if she really was Danjuma's daughter, well then, they might have trouble on their hands. He knew exactly who the man was and had no wish to go to war with him.

At least not yet.

For the moment there was enough room for both of them.

The time would come when there wouldn't be, but that wasn't today. He summoned one of his men. "Put her somewhere safe and make sure you keep an eye on her. No one lays a finger on her, understood? We treat her as an honored guest."

"Sure, Boss," the man said and beckoned the girl to follow, but she showed no sign of doing so.

"Are you going to walk, or do I get him to carry you?"

"Is that how you treat an honored guest?" She said, her arms still folded across her chest.

"Just go with him, girl," Boss said.

She glared at him then followed the man.

He waited until she'd been led inside one of the outbuildings before he turned on the pair of idiots who'd brought her here.

"What the fuck were you thinking? You brought Sol Danjuma's daughter here? Do you know who the fuck he is?"

They both shrugged. "Should we?" Daudi asked. "We found her in Lebna's apartment. The one he shared with his mysterious girlfriend. We thought it might be her."

"Well, it obviously isn't, unless he was into fucking children."

"It all went so fast. We didn't really get a good look at her until we were well on our way here."

"And you didn't think to stop the car and let her go?"

"We thought…"

"No!" Boss interrupted. "If you'd thought you wouldn't have gone into town in the first place."

"But she might know something."

"She might, but do you think that finding out if she does is worth starting a war over?"

"A war?"

"Yes. A goddamned war. Her father runs this town. If he comes looking for her, we will be drawn into something we can't finish. You understand the concept of being worm food, right? Fucking idiots. Now get the fuck out of my sight while I try to think how to get us out of this shit you've just rained down on our heads."

He watched the pair of them slink away, heads hung low. They didn't exchange a single word with anyone. If they had any sense, the idiots would stay in their bunks for the rest of the day. But they'd already established they had no fucking sense.

"Fuck," Boss grunted, this time so softly barely anyone heard. They didn't need to. Everyone around him knew *exactly* what was going through his mind.

He needed to talk to the girl and work out how he was going to get her back home before too much damage was done. And if that wasn't doable, whether he was going to have to take more drastic action.

As loathe as he was to admit it, those two knuckle draggers had linked Danjuma to Lebna's death. He couldn't let that go without some kind of response.

He needed to think. The problem was he didn't have a lot of time to do it.

Danjuma would already be looking for his little girl.

"Maybe she doesn't know where she is?" Kanda Mulai said coming up to his side. "We could blindfold her and dump her on the other side of Freetown without her knowing where she'd been taken to?"

"There are landmarks on the drive out here," he was thinking of the old oil depot. Those towering drums were hard to miss and harder to mistake.

"Danjuma is a smart man. He's not going to start something if he already has his daughter back unharmed. The potential damage to his operation from full-scale war would be massive. Maybe we can even turn that to our advantage; tell him that we know that he was involved in Lebna's death and tell him that things could have been a lot worse. We could have taken an eye for an eye, but we chose not to. We chose to give him the warning—and will accept his tribute. Give us the boy's killer and we will call it even."

"Perhaps," Boss said.

He'd known the old man all his life and he valued his counsel. He was wise in ways a lot of his crew were not, simply because he had lived through so much death, pain, and suffering. But this was a decision he had to make for himself.

He would speak to the girl.

Boss hated being pushed into a corner like this, forced into making a decision without enough time to consider the implications. He was a thoughtful man, not prone to rash actions. Rash actions cost lives and livelihoods. He patted the old man on the shoulder then headed off in search of the girl.

If she was going to be taken back, he was going to be the one to do it, and if she was going to be put down, well then that fell to him too.

They had the sense to take her to the kitchen rather than lock her up somewhere.

His guard stood by the door while she sat at the Formica table drumming her finger on the fake wood. A glass of orange juice was on the table beside her hand.

"You can go," he told the guard, before taking a seat opposite the girl.

In the artificial light it was easy to see how the idiots had mistaken her for someone older. She dressed like someone who was closer to twenty than to twelve, but no one knew better than him just how deceptive appearances could be.

"So, you're the boss?" she asked.

"I am," he said. "But it is just Boss."

There was still that veiled aggression in her voice, but it had been tempered by the few minutes she'd spent alone. She was beginning to appreciate the situation she found herself in, and that daddy couldn't always get her out of a hole.

"But you're in charge here," she said. "Wherever here is."

"I am."

"So, what are you planning on doing to me?"

To me, not with. She expected pain, maybe rape, probably death. "That depends."

"On what?"

"On the next few minutes. I would like you to answer a few questions for me."

"But I don't know anything," she said.

"Let me be the judge of that. For a start, I'd like to know what you were doing at the apartment."

"Lebna's place?"

"Yes. Lebna's place. You know Lebna then?"

She shook her head. "Not me," she said, then corrected herself. "Well, I've met him a couple of times, but I don't know him."

Don't, not didn't.

"Then why were you there?"

She gave a heavy sigh then leaned forward on the table. "He's my sister's boyfriend. They were supposed to be moving in together, that was meant to be their place... she can't get hold of him... she's worried about him. Me, I thought he had another girl, so I thought we could try and catch them," she mimed a gesture of bodies fucking with her hands.

"And you sister... when did she last see him?"

Another shrug. "Couple of days ago, maybe three. I don't know all the ins and outs of my sister's love life you know."

The more he listened to her, the more he found himself liking the girl She was feisty. And smart. And that might make things difficult further along the line.

He nodded. "Let me ask you something... Do you have any idea what Lebna does for me?" he was careful to keep it in the present tense.

"He won't tell Dana what he does, but I think he's involved in drugs."

Boss sniffed. "What makes you think that?"

"Just a feeling," she said, and he couldn't help but think she was deliberately trying to sound more worldly than she was. "You get to know the signs when you've spent enough time around people in that world."

"Like your father?"

She didn't bother denying it.

It wasn't her father he wanted to talk about, it was Lebna.

"So, you don't have any idea where Lebna might have gone? Any friends he had in town?"

Lori shook her head. "Dana told me he didn't know many people. I don't think she knew much about him, to be honest. She never mentioned friends or family, nor this place."

Why would she, Boss thought to himself. This girl was the first outsider they'd brought here since they'd set up home in the compound.

"What about your father?"

"What about him?"

"Does he know Lebna?"

"No. Dana wasn't ready for them to meet."

Boss nodded. "How did he feel about that?"

"I don't know. I'm not a mind reader. Why so many questions? I want to go home now."

"I want you to go home, too," he said as possibilities started to come together in his mind. "But I need to find out what happened to Lebna."

"I've told you everything I know. He'll turn up sooner or later."

"Oh, he already has," Boss told her.

"He's here? Then why have you got me trapped in here?" Lori asked, her face a mass of confusion.

"Because he's dead. Someone dumped his body at our door. And what they had done to him… it was ugly."

CHAPTER
SEVENTEEN

Danjuma was in no mood to talk when Connors finally got to see him.

Everything was slipping through his fingers.

With every hour the drugs were further and further away from him and there was nothing he could do about it. No drugs, no money to pay back his investors, no future. It was a simple equation.

"And just what do you expect me to do?" Danjuma asked. "This is not my problem. I don't have to do shit for you. If I do, it's as a favor. If you can raise the money, I can sell you another consignment. I will even give you a discount, just to see the back of your skinny white ass."

"But…"

"There are no buts in this situation. I've got more important things to deal with at the moment."

"Well maybe I can help. You know, quid pro quo…"

"Quid pro quo? What the fuck is that supposed to mean? You've been watching too many damned movies, American. Maybe that's how you got yourself in this shit. Not enough sense of the real world."

"It means that if I help you, you help me."

"I know what the words mean, I am not ignorant just because I live in Africa. What I don't know, is what you think *you* can do that my men can't? Do you have some kind of superpower that can help me get my daughter back?"

"Your daughter?"

"None of your concern," he said. "There's nothing you can do, and now I'm not even sure why I had you brought here. I don't have the energy to deal with you."

"You said…"

"I know what I said. I changed my mind." He paused to think for a moment, trying to decide what he should do with the American. There was still an argument to be made that he might come in useful somehow, but Danjuma didn't know how yet. Yet. That was a powerful word in his life. It meant would, eventually. And for the time being that meant it was smart to keep the American close.

If he became a nuisance, he would deal with him later.

"I'll get someone to take you to one of the guest rooms, then someone will bring you something to eat and drink. I suggest you stay out of my way until I call for you."

Danjuma stepped out of the room and went in search of Rakeem.

It didn't take long to find the man in the kitchen, nursing a mug of coffee. There was a sheen of sweat on the big man's face, but there was nothing unusual about that.

"Thanks for bringing him in," Danjuma said. "Even if he is just another headache."

Rakeem nodded. "Indeed. Aren't they always? Americans. Headaches." He smiled. "I hear I missed something more important?"

"It's hard to keep secrets in a place like this."

"It's all everyone is talking about," Rakeem agreed. "No one has even asked me why I brought that white guy here. It's all about Lori."

Danjuma would have preferred it if the American had been the talk of the house.

"So, my friend, tell me, what do you know about this boy my daughter was seeing?"

"I've already told you everything there is to tell. I reported back every time they met."

"I know, and I appreciate it. Always looking out for the family, your loyalty does not go unnoticed, old friend." Rakeem smiled. "But what about when they *weren't* together?"

From the day he had learned that Dana was seeing the boy he had asked Rakeem to keep an eye on them, and to find out everything he could about the boy, look for weaknesses and lies, things that betrayed some ulterior motive for homing in on his girl. It paid to know who was moving into your circle.

"What do you want to know?"

"The basics, where did he go? Who did he see? That sort of thing."

"He made a few trips out of town, but I couldn't follow him too far without tipping my hand. I didn't want him realizing he was being followed."

"Same direction each time?"

"Yeah, out past the old oil refinery. Towards the border. Some days, he was the only vehicle on the road, following him any further would have meant a blind man would see me behind him."

Danjuma nodded. He trusted Rakeem. The man was like a brother to him, with long years of loyal service. He wasn't some green-horn idiot. But that left one huge question dangling. Danjuma voiced it. "So, where the fuck is he now? He can't have just disappeared."

Rakeem shrugged. "Somewhere. Because he can't be nowhere. Maybe he is fucking around behind the girl's back?"

"Which you would have seen, wouldn't you? So no, not that. Next question, why were those guys at Lebna's apartment?"

"Easier to answer, I think. Looking for something?"

Danjuma nodded. It made sense. That was the way his mind had been going. "But why take Lori?" Because that bit didn't make sense. He shook his head. "Okay. Okay. I think we need to find wherever Lebna went to when he gave you the slip."

"He didn't give me the slip," Rakeem bristled.

Danjuma stopped him. "Sorry," he said, raising a hand. "Bad choice of words. You did the right thing in letting him go, but we have to find out where he went."

"Leave it to me. How is Dana? Is she okay?"

"Shaken, for sure."

"Want me to talk to her?"

The offer took Danjuma by surprise. "Why do you think she would tell you something that she wouldn't tell me?"

Rakeem shrugged. "Sometimes there are things a daughter might not want her father to know."

Which was true and without a mother in her life it made sense she'd look to replace that role with someone she'd known her entire life, even if it was a thug like Rakeem. He nodded. "I guess it can't do any harm, but not now. Leave her for a while. Show me where Lebna went, and how far you followed him. I think I will take a drive out later while you have a chat with Dana."

"Of course," Rakeem said and fished out his phone.

CHAPTER
EIGHTEEN

"What do you think he's going to do?" Musa asked.

He seemed to be getting more nervous by the minute.

As far as they knew, Boss was still speaking to the girl.

He was going out of his mind trying to guess how that was going.

Daudi lay on his bunk while Musa paced the room, making sure that neither of them settled. He didn't have an answer to the question, and he wasn't even sure if his friend expected one.

"This doesn't feel good, Daudi."

"There's nothing we can do about it," Daudi said.

"What if he decides that we can't afford to let her go? What if bringing her back here gets her killed?"

"Then it gets her killed," Daudi said. He'd tried not to think about that possibility, but it was there at the back of his mind. Boss was more than capable of making a drastic decision if he felt cornered.

Or if he decided her blood would avenge Lebna.

"We should do something. Say something."

"What can we do? We can't go in there when he's with her... he would kill us for it..."

Any further musing on their fate and whether they should intervene was ended by the door opening. A figure stood in the opening. "He wants to see you both. Now."

Neither of them hesitated. Daudi was off his bunk and out the door a second behind Musa. Not wanting to make things worse by making Boss wait, they hurried to the kitchen. Boss was just coming out of the room when they reached him. There was a moment where they didn't know what they were rushing into, and then relief swept through them as Boss said, "She knows nothing. She doesn't even know Lebna is dead."

"What?" said Daudi. "How can she not know?"

Boss gave a grunt. "Why would you think she would? Or did you think that little girl killed him and dumped his body at our gates?"

"Of course not, but I thought..."

Boss cut him off. "I am fed up with hearing that word coming out of your mouth, Daudi. The pair of you have got us in a hole full of shit with the man who runs that fucking town shoveling it down on our heads. When he finds out that you two are behind his daughter's kidnap you are both dead men. So, tell me now, who saw you? We need to limit the damage here. If we can."

"Nobody," Musa insisted, finding his voice.

Boss raised an eyebrow but said nothing for a moment. He turned his gaze to Daudi.

"A couple of shopkeepers," he said. "Maybe one or two people in the street..."

"And her fucking sister," Boss added.

"Sister?"

"Yes, her sister. The one Lebna was screwing. You two idiots didn't even realize that there were two girls in that apartment? I despair. You two are braindead... The older sister got out first... you left her in the street, watching you as you grabbed this one. She saw you, saw your car, and which way you went. Even if the others didn't realize what was going on, she did. I would bet your lives their father is already hunting you."

"But he doesn't know we're here," Musa said, desperation creeping into his voice.

"You think not? Are we, perhaps, invisible? We have moved into his territory. We have taken trade from his table, money from his pocket. He knows who we are and where we are. This will be the first place Sol Danjuma comes looking for you."

"You want us to leave?" Daudi asked. It was the logical thing to demand, exile for them, and better than the alternative, turning them over to Danjuma for punishment.

He glanced at Musa to see a mixture of confusion and panic on his face.

It was an offer that he hoped Boss would refuse.

Daudi offered up an alternative. "We should take the girl back to her father and apologize, throw ourselves on his mercy."

"That might save me a whole lot of trouble," Boss agreed. "But in his place, I can't imagine being forgiving. I send you to him, I am throwing you to the wolves."

"We'll take out chances." Daudi said.

It was just bravado.

He was saying the things he thought that Boss wanted to hear.

But at the same time, he was praying he wouldn't take them up on it.

If he went back into the town, he was a dead man.

And so was Musa.

Boss grunted again. "You two can babysit her while I decide what we're going to do." He didn't condemn them, but it was a long way from salvation. Boss walked away from them. Daudi glanced at Musa and saw a look of relief on his face that mirrored his own.

Daudi led the way into the dining room. It was a grand title for the place that they ate—a room with half a dozen Formica-topped tables surrounded by a mismatched assortment of chairs. Everything in the room had seen better days, apart from the girl.

She might be young, Daudi thought, but add a few years and it wasn't hard to see why Lebna had fallen for her sister.

"You two morons again?" she said. "Come to take me home then?"

"Can I get you anything?" Daudi asked, ignoring her barbed jibe.

"Ah, so you've been reduced to room service? You really did fuck up, didn't you?" She slouched back in her chair; arms folded in front of her.

"Something like that," Daudi said. "Look, you don't have to believe me, but I'm sorry about this. Lebna was my friend. I didn't mean to scare you."

The girl smiled and suddenly any tension in the room disappeared. Daudi hated himself. If Boss couldn't find a way out of this, she would be dead soon. And it would all be his fault.

CHAPTER
NINETEEN

Rakeem had tried to tell Danjuma not to go out alone, but he was having none of it.

The big man told him which road he'd seen Lebna driving when he had left the city, and where he'd been forced to peel off and leave him.

It had been a long time since Sol Danjuma had last been out this way, but very little had changed.

He enjoyed driving, even it wasn't something he did a lot of. Hell, furthest he had driven himself recently was across town to see Dominique. He couldn't have said why. It wasn't that he felt unsafe in the city he called his own; no one would dare mess with him. But then, he'd thought that about his girls, too.

In the end he'd relented and given in to Rakeem's protests, agreeing not to go alone. Hence he was accompanied by one of the younger errand boys he had working out of the house. He wore a handgun in a breast holster, an unnecessary precaution for two men taking a nice afternoon drive. His name was Keno—at least was what Danjuma *thought* it was, he wasn't going to ask him and prove himself wrong.

Buildings thinned out the further he drove from the center until he reached a collection of ramshackle structures that had sprung up alongside the road like weeds.

"Who are these people?" Danjuma asked, confused by the shantytown that seemed to have sprung up around his dominion.

"Foreigners mainly," Keno grunted with disdain. "Illegals. They don't belong here. They came over the border thinking that they would find a better life here, that they would be safer, and they end up in this shit hole. You can't tell me this is better than where they came from."

Danjuma felt his skin creep. "How long have they been here?" Places like this don't just spring up overnight, he thought.

"A year, maybe more. There was a whole wave of them when the war broke out. Now they're everywhere."

Danjuma couldn't believe that he'd been so ignorant about the pilot fish clinging to the shark of his city. He knew that refugees had come across the border, seeking asylum, but not that they'd settled here, on the edge of town, and made a life for themselves.

They passed the last of the makeshift houses where a young couple and an old man were wrestling with a tent while the desert wind made life difficult for them.

He was tempted to suggest that they help, but Keno's hand had moved to the grip of his weapon.

"You expect trouble from these people?" Danjuma asked.

"I don't trust them," Keno said. "Someone took your daughter. It could easily be these people. She could even be here."

Danjuma thought about it for a moment, then shook his head. "I don't think so. Rakeem's description of things had them driving until they were out in open country. He followed this far, if not further, so no, this isn't where they took her."

"That doesn't mean that these people aren't the ones who took Lina," Keno argued.

Danjuma drummed his hands on the steering wheel, toying with the idea of stopping and talking to some of these people, but as he slowed, he saw the look in their eyes as they looked back at him.

There was a level of desperation here that felt dirty, but looking at their faces one after another he couldn't see any of them snatching his daughter from Lebna's apartment. There was just no logical reason for it.

He kept driving until they had left the last of the shantytown behind.

The road fell into disrepair. The border had been closed for the best part of a year so there was little cause for traffic.

"How far to the border?" he asked, considering the possibility that Dana's boy had been crossing the border.

But why would he be doing that?

He dug his fingernails into the steering wheel, angry that he knew so little about the boy who had been about to set up home with his daughter.

He might have had Kareem following him, and even had his apartment checked at one point, but he'd learned nothing of value about the boy. When he found him, Danjuma resolved, he was going to tie him to a chair and slap all seven shades out of him until he had learned every last thing there was to know about him, and then slap him some more for upsetting his daughter.

And if he didn't get Lori back safe and sound, he was going to make his life a living hell for as long as it lasted. Which wouldn't be long.

Keno didn't answer him straight away, but when Danjuma glanced across he saw the young errand runner was checking his phone. "Another twenty miles," he said. "I don't think I've ever been this close to it."

"Never?"

Keno shrugged. "Why would I? What's on the other side that's better than what we have here?"

"The sea, if you drive far enough," Danjuma laughed. "Maybe we should send you on the next run."

"There has to be an easier way of getting a shipment out of the country than driving through the middle of a warzone."

"Not when both factions are more than happy to let us through while we grease their palms.

"Still not my idea of fun."

"You are young. Think of all the exotic lovelies you could get at the coast."

Keno grunted. "Pox-ridden whores sharing diseases from around the world? I'll stay here, thanks."

"And lie with ugly local girls who only have local diseases," Danjuma finished for him. "Variety is the spice of life."

Keno didn't answer.

He slipped his phone back into his pocket and stared at the road ahead. Danjuma knew he'd touched a raw nerve. He let it go.

Off to their left, some distance away, Danjuma saw a group of buildings. He pulled to the side of the road, though he could just as well have stopped in the middle.

They hadn't encountered a single other vehicle since they left town.

He turned the engine off and got out of the car.

As he stood there, leaning against the car, the only sound came from the car engine, ticking as it cooled down.

He breathed deeply.

The air was fresher than it was in town.

He tried to remember when he had last done this; it would have been when the girls had been much younger, he realized, when he had taken them to see what lay beyond the last of the houses. While they had been in awe of the wide-open space at first, they had quickly grown bored and wanted to go home.

"It's an old army base," he told Keno as the other man slid out of the car.

"I didn't know there was an army base out here. You'd have thought we'd have seen soldiers and stuff, not just a few border guards coming and going."

"It wasn't one of ours. It was one of theirs."

"Why would they have a base on this side of the border?

"Because," Danjuma explained. "By the end of the last war the border had moved. Part of the peace settlement was that they cleared everything out."

"What, they left their shit behind?"

Danjuma shook his head. "No, they would have taken everything, and most likely set fire to the place."

"It's still standing."

"Concrete is resilient."

"I see smoke," Keno pointed.

"Which means people are living there again," Danjuma agreed. "I want to find out what's going on inside."

He saw the look on Keno's face.

"You want to drive straight up to the door and ask them what's going on?"

"Why not? I'm just a father looking for his missing daughter," he reasoned. "Why wouldn't I ask everywhere?"

CHAPTER
TWENTY

"Boss!" He was deep in thought when he heard the voice shouting his name.

"What the fuck do you want?" he grunted when the youth barged into his room. Of all the places in the camp, this was the one where no one entered without being invited first, even those closest to him.

"There's a car... Heading this way."

"And what the fuck do you expect me to do about it?"

"But after the last time..."

"That was a truck. Is this a truck?"

"No. It...."

"Is it speeding towards us as if the hounds of hell are on its back?"

"No, it's just driving towards us."

"Then do you want me to come out and hold your fucking hand? Or can you be trusted to deal with it yourself?"

He was already on his feet and slipping on his jacket.

He didn't need it; he never needed it, but it was like armor. He felt the weight of the gun he kept in the pocket.

———

Danjuma pulled the car to a halt a short distance from the huge double gates set into the outer wall of the compound and stared at it for a while.

Even if he hadn't known what this place had been in its previous life, up close he would have been able to guess. The place looked run down, with fire scars and patched up sections of breeze block filling what had once been holes in the wall.

"I don't know about you," said Keno, "but I have a bad feeling about this place."

Danjuma grunted.

Something told him that whoever had taken to squatting in there wasn't keen on visitors. That was enough to make him wary. And it convinced him they were in the right place.

"Now why would these people feel the need to post a couple of men on the walls?" He had already made their rifles. They were expecting trouble. Or if not expecting it, prepared for it.

"What the fuck do you want?" demanded a voice from the top of the wall. Danjuma had faced plenty of men like this one; emboldened by the gun in their hands and looking for an excuse to use it.

"Are you in charge?" Danjuma called up, calmly, but loud enough for his voice to carry.

"You're wasting your time."

"It's my time to waste. I'm looking for someone."

"What makes you think he's here?"

"What makes you think he isn't?" Danjuma took a few strides closer to the wall, partly so that he didn't have to shout, and partly so he could get a better look at the man. "Aren't you going to invite me in, so we don't have to keep on shouting?"

"Just fuck off will you. There's nothing for you here."

He took a risk, and said, "I'm looking for Lebna." He saw the man's expression change in an instant. It was a flicker, and didn't last for more than a heartbeat, but Danjuma saw it. At the mention of the name the man disappeared off the wall, no doubt running to tell who was really in charge, and that meant he'd come to the right place.

"No one called Lebna here," the other man fronted, ignoring the fact that his watch partner's disappearance into the compound contradicted every word coming out of his mouth. His grip on the rifle changed.

"You sure about that? Because I'm not sure I believe you."

The man shifted again. Sweat glistened on his forehead.

"There's no one called Lebna here," the man repeated, less certain this time. "Why are you so sure that he comes here?"

"He owes me," Danjuma said. "He promised me he had friends out here who would front him the debt, so I've come to collect."

"Naw, that's bullshit," the guard said, but before Danjuma could counter he stepped aside to let a hulk of a man take his place on the wall.

"Who the fuck are you?" the hulk said.

He had the aura of someone used to being obeyed.

"I'm looking for Lebna," he repeated.

"Maybe your hearing ain't so good. I asked, who the fuck are you?"

"Doesn't matter who I am? You're going to let me talk to Lebna, there's no more to say."

"There's no Lebna here, so just fuck off and don't bother coming back." He then turned away and disappeared out of sight.

Danjuma waited for a moment, just so he could see the guard step back onto the battlements and thrust out his chest with renewed bravado.

"You heard Boss," the guard said. "Now fuck the fuck off."

Danjuma knew that he could have given Keno the nod and he could have dropped him from this distance before the man had realized what was happening, but now wasn't the time.

He wanted to find out as much as he could about whatever went on behind those walls.

A wise man knew his enemy and learned everything there was to know about them so that when it came to breaking them there wasn't a bone left that didn't snap.

CHAPTER
TWENTY-ONE

Boss strode across the central courtyard to the sound of the engine firing up outside the wall.

He assumed the driver had taken the hint.

It unsettled him, though, that someone had come there looking for Lebna, but logic dictated the man out there hadn't been responsible for the boy's death. Otherwise, he would have strung them up, spread-eagle cuts through their flesh and left them hanging in the blistering sun as bird food.

It wasn't good that someone from the outside world knew they had settled in the old fortress.

The more people who knew about the place the more chance that others would come to the gates, either looking for refuge or retribution, that was just the way of their life. Right now, he wanted nothing more than peace while he waited for the consignment to come in. It was difficult to be patient with so much on the line. He was getting antsy. Itchy. Expecting things to go wrong, like Lebna had been a precursor of pain to come. But there were limits, even for someone like Boss. He could ride out the nerves and stare down threats. It was when this stuff progressed beyond that and put them at risk, that things needed to happen. He was prepared to abandon the compound if it came to the worst. There was always somewhere new for hermit crabs like him to settle.

The consignment was due to arrive tomorrow.

But he knew that tomorrow could just as easily mean the day after, given the complexities of transport. What he really didn't want was it taking longer than that. The greater the exposure, the greater the risk of things moving outside of his control, and Boss hated not being in control.

And the temperature of Freetown was changing, fast. There was an added element of urgency in the case of the girl, Danjuma's brat, and her fate.

Daudi hadn't even had the brains to blindfold her, so she knew exactly where they'd brought her, meaning she could lead a whole world of pain to their door if they let her go.

"Who do you think it was?" Elias asked.

"Somebody looking for Lebna," Boss told his righthand man. Elias was the one man he'd bring with him out of this hell if it came to running. He trusted him more than he trusted his own brother. But then, Boss's brother was a murdering whoreson who would sell their mother out for a sniff of poontang.

"Not the girl then?"

Boss shook his head. "Just Lebna. Reckoned he was owed money. Well, he ain't getting that back."

"Hmm, dunno, Boss, that doesn't sound like the Lebna I knew. He didn't rack up debts. The boys used to joke when they went into Freetown he wore his trousers with the pockets sewn up, so he didn't have to dip into his pocket for money."

Boss grinned. He'd heard the story before. "Maybe he borrowed some for that new place."

Elias shook his head. "Naw, he'd saved more than enough to cover the rent on the apartment for six months. He used to boast about it. I don't like it, Boss. Ain't no one he'd owe enough money to that'd drag them out here looking for him."

Boss nodded. The same doubt had been gnawing away at him for the last couple of minutes. "And ask yourself this, how did he know Lebna was one of ours? It isn't like the boy shouted his mouth off when it came to his allegiances."

Elias was one step ahead when it came to putting the pieces together. "But whoever dumped his body here knew he was."

Boss nodded; he couldn't disagree.

They had turned away plenty of those who had come over the border in search of safety, sending them down to the shantytown on the edge of Freetown. It wasn't going to be one of those. They knew better than to fuck with Boss and his people. But word had got out. It was always through someone going pussy-hunting in the city. There was always a red line that could be threaded through any set of circumstances, a joining of the metaphorical dots. So Lebna tells the girl he's shacking up with, the one whose sister was in the kitchen.

Whose father was...

"Sol Danjuma," Boss said.

Elias looked at him then and nodded slowly. "But why was he asking for Lebna, not his daughter?"

"Fucking with us? Letting us know he knew? Wanting us to know he'd left us a little present? Fuck."

But he'd seemed so calm; Boss tried to put himself in the other man's place, father to father, and imagine keeping his cool like that. And he couldn't do it. A man who could remain *that* calm was dangerous.

"Put a couple of extra men on watch tonight," he said. "There could be trouble."

Elias didn't need telling twice. The conversation was over.

Now, he needed to decide what the fuck to do with the girl.

CHAPTER
TWENTY-TWO

Danjuma was convinced of two things.

First, there was no doubt in his mind they had found the right place; this was where Lebna had come from.

Two, the guy on the wall was a poor liar, but that wasn't what he was hiding. That left Lori.

Whether they'd taken her, or she had gotten caught in some sort of grudge between them and someone else, it amounted to the same thing. The answers were inside that old fortress.

The problem was getting inside.

Keno talked as he drove, about nothing of real substance. Danjuma was able to block him out.

He needed to think.

After a while, his thoughts were caught in a never-ending spiral, going round and around without taking him anywhere. They were still at least twenty minutes from home. He checked his watch.

They had been gone for a couple of hours. And in all that time his phone had not rung once.

That was unusual.

That meant anything they had to tell him was either insignificant or bad. None of his people would want to deliver bad news through the phone. Bad news could almost always wait. But if there was bad news waiting, someone would have found a way to tell him to come back home.

Silence was unsettling.

He made the call home himself.

Dana snatched the phone up and asked a breathless, "Dad! Have you found her?" Before he could even say hello.

"Not yet, baby girl." He stopped himself then, realizing that he hadn't called her that in years. But she was still his baby girl, even though she was the oldest. "But I will. I promise you."

"How? Everyone's been looking, but there's no sign of her."

"I know where she is," he replied. "It's not as simple as I'd like," he said. "But I'll tell you all about it when I get back. Trust me, I'm bringing your sister home." He said his goodbyes and hung up.

He was already regretting making the call; he should have called Rakeem first, but what was done was done. He called Rakeem next. Like his daughter, the man answered straight away.

"Have you found her?" the man asked. The same question. How many ways could it be asked? How many times?

"Where are you?" Danjuma replied, ignoring the question.

"In the kitchen," Danjuma pictured his old friend nursing a cup of coffee and smoking a cigarette as if he had no worries in the world. It wasn't reality, he knew, but it was a nice illusion of it in his mind's eye.

"Dana tell you anything we didn't already know?"

"Not really. Bits and pieces about the boy, but nothing of any value. Did you find the place?"

"Yeah, I'm sure as shit that's where he came from, but I'm not so sure he's there now. But I've got the feeling Lori is."

There was silence for a moment then Rakeem said, "There's something else."

"Go on."

"The other American has turned up. He was still in town."

"The double crosser? Do I want to be bothered with this or can it be dealt with? Nah, fuck it, tell me, where the hell did you find him?"

"Holed up in a motel."

"And the consignment? Did you recover that, too?"

"Every last gram."

"Now why the hell didn't the stupid fuck just get as far away from here as he could?"

"He's not talking... but he will." The pause was enough to tell Danjuma exactly how the information was going to be extracted. Painfully. "Thing is, we found a map on him, and wouldn't you just know it, the old fort you've just been to is marked out on it."

Danjuma let that sink in, then slowly smiled. "Now that is interesting. Where is he now?"

"At the club. Thought it best to keep him out of the way. A couple of the guys are with him. He won't be going anywhere."

"You said anything to Connors?"

"No. You want me to?"

"Not yet. He can stew a little longer while we decide what we're going to do."

"What do you want to do?"

"I think I'd like to get his side of the story. I'll meet you at the club."

"You want me to bring anyone else?" Meaning Connors, and as tempting as that was, it would turn it into an unnecessary sideshow.

"Just the two of us for now."

Danjuma ended the call without saying goodbye, there was no need. The conversation was over. If the American knew anything about what was going on behind those walls, Danjuma was going to make sure he told him, no matter what it took.

CHAPTER
TWENTY-THREE

The girl seemed remarkably calm given her situation.

Boss stood in the doorway and watched her for a couple of minutes.

If she betrayed any emotion at all it was more akin to boredom than fear. If boredom was even an emotion.

"How long are you thinking of keeping me here?" She asked eventually, releasing a heavy sigh.

"That depends," Boss said.

"On what? On whether my father pays a ransom for me? That's never going to happen. You may as well just let me go now and miss out all the crap."

"Do you know what happens to little girls whose father don't pay the ransom?" He asked, watching her face for the slightest reaction. There wasn't so much of a flicker. "They don't get to go home."

"What the fuck you talking about?"

"You have a dirty mouth, don't you?"

She looked away, caught out for a moment, but didn't speak.

"You ought to know, your father was just here." This time he saw the reaction, a sudden light in her eyes as she looked up at him.

"What did he say?"

"He was only interested in that poor kid, Lebna. Or at least he said he was."

"Does he know I'm here?"

"Why would he? But what I'm curious about is why he'd come here looking for a dead boy and not mention you?"

She hadn't known that Lebna was dead, so there was a good chance her father didn't know either. But if that was the case, then Danjuma wasn't behind his murder, and if he wasn't, who was? The questions buzzed like flies around his mind.

"Maybe you can help me with something, girl. Tell me, how well did you know Lebna?"

"I didn't," she said, not missing a beat. "Not well. I met him a couple of times, that's all. He was my sister's boyfriend."

"Someone killed him," he said. "And I want to know who."

"It wasn't me," she said.

"I never for a moment thought it was. I can't see you dumping his body outside our gates like you're dropping off the trash. But I'm wondering, is that the kind of thing your father would do?"

"Daddy?" She shook her head. "Why would you think he could do such a thing?"

"Danjuma has quite the reputation."

"He's a well-respected businessman."

Boss laughed at that. "I guess that's one way of looking at it."

"And what do mean by that?" she said, bristling. There was no hiding the anger in her voice.

Boss folded his arms across his chest and leaned against the door frame. "How do you think your father makes his money?"

"He's a businessman."

"He is indeed, but what kind of business? That's a bigger question."

She shrugged. "He owns a club, and he buys and sells stuff."

"And, my dear child, now we find ourselves at the crux of things. What kinds of stuff might that be?"

She gave a shrug. "All kinds of stuff. Why so many questions?"

"I just wanted to see if you knew what kind of man your father is."

"I do. He's a good man," she said, but there was a difference between a good man around his daughters and a good man in a world of violence. He wondered if she really understood that.

Boss grunted.

The temptation was to push a little further, but he had no great appetite for breaking the girl. She was a child, whatever her father was or wasn't. Whether she knew what he did made no difference. Boss knew enough about Danjuma to know he wouldn't hesitate to use force to get his daughter back. The only thing protecting them from his anger were these walls.

He needed to make contingency plans.

CHAPTER
TWENTY-FOUR

The door to the club was open but there were no revelers inside.

One of the barmen was busy behind the bar setting things up for the night to come, checking bottles and polishing glasses. There was music playing, but it was quieter, and not the kind of wild meltdown that would be played later in the evening.

"Rakeem?" Danjuma asked.

"Downstairs," the barmen nodded towards the cellar doorway, barely pausing in his work.

Danjuma came around the back of the bar and opened the door to the cellar. The light was already turned on, illuminating a stone staircase down. He half-expected to hear voices, but there was only silence down there.

He closed the door behind him.

He could no longer hear the music.

The isolation was that good. No sound made it down. No sound made it back up.

Unusually he'd find himself distracted by the racks of wine and rare spirits, the casks of imported beers, and other stuff in this treasure trove of debauchery, but today none of it held the least bit of interest for him.

He was focused solely on the door at the far end of the storage room. It was a large, imposing slab of metal that seemed so out of place against the more archaic racks of booze in the dusty cellar, like something in a meat storage locker. He took a breath before he reached out for the handle, then swung it open.

The man sat on a chair in the middle of the room.

His head was slumped down.

Danjuma didn't need to see his face to know that he'd taken a beating.

He would have liked to have been there for it.

"He wasn't keen on being tied up," Rakeem observed, seeing the boss come in. Danjuma hadn't registered his presence, despite knowing that he was in room. He was a wraith. Danjuma turned to see his red right hand leaning against the wall looking bored, like there was no fun in the torture anymore.

On the other side of the door stood the two men who had brought the American here.

They were no doubt responsible for the state of the man, though no doubt Rakeem had thrown a few punches for good measure.

Danjuma tipped his head towards the door. "Take a break," he said. "You've done good."

He saw the bucket in the corner but didn't pick it up until the two men had left and closed the door behind them. He didn't know if it was water or piss inside, and to be honest didn't case. He threw the contents at the man, who came alert in a heartbeat, spitting and gasping for air.

"You're lucky," Danjuma said.

"Lucky?" The man spat.

"Oh yes, believe me," Danjuma said as the man licked at his dry and cracked lips. "You could be dead already."

"What's this all about?" the man fronted.

"Don't fuck with me," Danjuma said, bluntly. "You're not looking quite as cocky as the last time we met."

"The last time?" The man said and looked at Danjuma, his swollen eyes struggling to focus. Then realization struck. He knew who he was looking at.

"You."

"Me," he agreed. "I've got your ex-partner, too. He's in my spare bedroom waiting for me to decide what the fuck I'm going to do with the pair of you. I don't like trouble, Mr. American. On the contrary, I am a big fan of a quiet life. So, what I need to decide is what course of action gives me the peace and quiet I crave."

"Fuck," the man in the chair said.

"Fuck indeed," said Danjuma and glanced across at Rakeem. "What do you think we should do with him?"

Rakeem pulled a handgun out of the waistband of his jeans and held it up. "I have an idea." The man in the chair glanced his way, a flash of fear in his eyes; and it was probably the first moment of real fear he'd betrayed, even during the beating. Rakeem pressed the barrel against the side of his head.

"Please," the man said. "Just tell me what you want. Whatever it is, you want it, you've got it."

Danjuma motioned with his head for Rakeem to step aside.

The man was frightened enough, push him too far and he would break down. It was all about keeping him on the right side of sheer terror, that place where he could still apply more pressure when it was needed.

"Tell me about the drugs," Danjuma said.

"We bought them from you. Is that what you want? You want them back, you can have them, just let me go."

"Don't treat me like I'm stupid, just because of the color of my skin. I don't like that. I won't treat you like a stupid fuck if you don't treat me like one. Besides, they aren't yours to give back, I already have them. Now, let me explain your new reality to you. Rakeem here would be more than happy to put a bullet in your head, nice and quick. He is a pragmatic soul. It isn't difficult to clean up blood. Easier than a lot of other messes, if you get what I mean."

The man looked up again and this time there was something different in his eyes—a pleading had joined the fear.

If Danjuma promised him his freedom in return for him leaving this cellar, going to his own mother's house and killing her, he would have done it, no question. The man was desperate.

"Tell me what you were going to do with the consignment you stole from your partner. I know you had no intention of honoring the deals your partner had put in place."

The man shook his head, then winced, clearly regretting it. "No, I'd lined something up myself. It might not have been as much as the original deal, but then I wouldn't have been splitting it with anyone else, so it was more in my pocket."

"Well, you are an honest man, if not a smart one," Danjuma said.

The man paused for a moment, looking Danjuma in the eyes.

Danjuma knew that he was weighing up his options, wondering if by telling him everything it would get him out of there, or just mean he got the bullet in the head that much quicker. It was exactly what Danjuma would have been thinking in his place. And then there was the second question, would betraying his new buyer in the old fortress get him killed even if he walked out of here?

"I haven't got all fucking day," Danjuma said, his voice steady and level, no trace of anger in it despite the profanity. He was facing a man who knew that he had lost everything.

"I had a buyer," he said.

"I know you did. What is his name?"

The man shrugged. "They just call him Boss."

"And where were you supposed to meet this Boss? Was he buying the stuff off you, or just helping you get it out of the country?"

"Buying it," the man said. He tried to sit up a little straighter, but it wasn't easy with his injuries.

"Where was the buy going down?"

"There's some kind of settlement a few miles out of town, an old army base or something. I've got a map."

Danjuma nodded. "And you were just supposed to drive up to the place, give Boss the stuff, and he'd give you your money? Is that how it was supposed to work?"

The man nodded. Another grimace.

"Okay, so tell me, what is stopping this Boss from putting a bullet in your brain, taking your consignment and burying you in the desert?"

"A contact vouched for him. Said he'd play it straight as long as I didn't try to screw him over."

"Who's the contact?"

"A guy named Clint Eastwood. We were in the army together."

Danjuma roared with laughter. "Clint muthafucking Eastwood? Are you shitting me, man?"

There was a moment of panic, with the man frantically, and painfully, shaking his head. "No, no, his real name is Norm... Norm Eastwood... we just called him Clint."

"Clint fucking Eastwood."

The man in the chair tried to join in on the laughter, but his was forced and hollow.

"And how does Clint know this Boss?" Danjuma asked.

"He did some kind of job for him, not sure what. Clint stays pretty tight-lipped when it comes to his work."

"And what type of work does Clint do?"

"Private security," the man said.

"Here, or in America?"

"All over the world," he said, "but he's worked over here a lot."

"Ah, a mercenary," Danjuma almost spat out the word. It wasn't enough that men were killing each other in one country after another, they had to bring in foreigners to help with the job.

The man tried to shrug, as if forgetting that his arms were still restrained, and failed miserably. "He said that him and his men have some heavy weaponry."

"And he was going to buy the drugs off you." It was a statement, not a question, confirming that he had it clear in his head. "What else do you know about this man you were dealing with?"

The American licked his lips. He broke eye contact. "He said I could pick up some extra cash if I picked up a few young girls for him along the way."

"Young girls? Just how young are we talking?" Danjuma felt his heart beating louder and faster, fear and anger threatening to spill over. There were many dark things in this world he would do, without a second thought, but there were others he would not tolerate.

"Ten, twelve, maybe a little older, but only if they look young."

Danjuma felt his mouth dry up. It was hard to remain calm as he asked, "And what does he want them for?" when he already knew the answer.

The man looked up again. "He sells them overseas."

The anger spilled over.

Danjuma swung his right hand, knuckles thundering into the man's face. His head snapped back, spit and blood flying.

When the American finally looked back he appeared dazed, his eyes unable to focus. There was a deep cut on his cheek where Danjuma's gold signet ring ripped through the flesh to the bone.

It wasn't that Danjuma was angry with the man in front of him, but his rage had to go somewhere, and that somewhere was into the American's face.

His daughter had fallen into the hands of sex traffickers.

The thought churned his gut.

He was ready to go to war, blazing with righteous fury.

He'd burn the whole fucking compound down and stand over the smoldering corpses making damned sure each and every one of the sick bastards melted in the flames.

He needed to get his little girl out of that place.

Every paternal instinct welled up, swarming through his mind, and robbing him of anything approaching sense.

He clenched his fist, ready to swing again.

He bit on the inside of his lip, tasting blood.

He unclenched his fist, stretching his fingers wide.

Force was a mistake when cunning would be far more effective. He needed to play to his strengths. There was a reason he had become king of Freetown and it wasn't that he'd run headlong into fights without knowing the extent of the threat waiting for him.

"When are they expecting you?"

"Tomorrow, maybe the day after."

"Which?" Danjuma demanded.

"Either," the American said. "We left it vague to allow for unforeseen circumstances. The agreement was that I needed to drop it off at their door before the end of the month or the deal was off."

"How will they know it's you?"

"It's not complicated. I just have to say who I am, give them Clint's name, and they open the gate."

Danjuma thought about it for a moment, considering the possibilities. "So, what's stopping me from taking your place?"

"You want the truth?"

Danjuma nodded.

"Look at me, then look at yourself in the mirror, what's the one thing that strikes you as different?"

"You are a white man."

CHAPTER
TWENTY-FIVE

There had to be a way to use Connors to get inside that base.

That was the smart move.

The problem was he couldn't trust the man to carry it through; he was a coward, and the moment he was inside he'd try to would use the drugs to broker a better deal with this Boss to get his ass out of Freetown and as far away from him as possible. Danjuma knew it. He knew people.

The only answer was sending someone in there with him; someone that Boss and his men wouldn't suspect, someone who would be able to get done whatever needed to be done and look after himself.

There was only one person he could think of.

He'd left Rakeem with instructions to get the American cleaned up and given something to eat and drink, but not let him out of his sight.

Then he arranged for a couple of men to head up to the old army base and keep an eye on the place from a safe distance, but not to be seen. If anyone came out of there, he wanted to know about it.

Now he sat in his car, his fingers drumming on the steering wheel.

He needed to make a call, and he needed to do it right.

It was answered on the second ring.

"Hey babe," Dominique said. "What's up? I wasn't expecting to hear from you until later."

"Ah well, somethings come up and I need a favor."

"Anything, you know that," she said.

"Probably better if I tell you in person," he said.

"You know I won't say no to you," There was a laugh in her voice, but he still wasn't sure about asking for her help.

"It's not that," he said. "Honestly, it'll be easier for you to say no if we are face to face."

"No hints?"

"I'd rather wait," he said.

"Well, okay, it all sounds very mysterious though," she laughed. "I'm out at the moment but I can be at the apartment in about twenty minutes if that works for you? But I won't be able to stay."

"I won't need long."

"I'll see you in twenty minutes."

He hung up.

He hated having to ask her, and wouldn't blame her if she said no.

It was his daughter who was in trouble, not hers, and she would be the one risking her life to bring Lori home. If she said yes.

He turned on the engine, glanced in the mirrors and pulled away from the side of the road.

It would only take him ten minutes to get to the apartment.

Months ago, he had given her a key to the place, but she had never used it. She always waited for him to arrive first. There was still a distance between them, a barrier that kept his life with her separate from his daughters. Things were going to change now, though. They would have to if he was going to see Lori again.

Dominique arrived a few minutes after him.

"It's my daughter," he said, as he closed the door behind them. "She's been kidnapped." And then it all came out. She didn't interrupt him, didn't ask any questions until he'd told her everything. Even then she sat in silence for a moment, thinking before she spoke.

"What do you need me to do?"

"I have a guy who's supposed to be delivering a consignment of cocaine to the people who've got her."

"You trust him?"

Danjuma had already asked himself the same question more times than he could count. "Maybe. My thinking is if he walks in and tells them he's taken someone with him to get my baby girl out, he's likely to get himself killed."

"And me," she said. "I assume that's the favor you wanted to ask me."

"You're ahead of me," he said, but he nodded. "He's a white guy, and if I go in there, or one of my guys, it's going to be pretty fucking obvious things aren't right."

"But they won't see a woman as a threat," she reasoned. "People always underestimate the women."

"Like I said," Danjuma said.

"So, you want me to go in there and get your girl out? Do I want to know how I'm supposed to do that?"

"You don't have to. Just get the doors open for me when I need them opened. If you can cause some kind of diversion, even better. I'll do the rest."

"What kind of vehicle are we going in with?"

"Not sure, I think he's driving a pile of junk, but we'd better still use it."

"How soon?"

"Tomorrow," Danjuma said.

"That doesn't give us a lot of time."

At no point had she said she wasn't going to do it or question the risk. But he still needed to hear her say the words aloud.

"So?"

She nodded. "Can you get me the car and a workshop for a couple of hours tonight?"

"Of course," Danjuma said. "What do you need?"

"Any repair shop will be fine."

"Anything else?"

She shook her head. "I can put my hands on everything else."

"You won't be able to carry a gun in there with you," he said.

"Trust me," she said. "With what I'm planning to wear there would be nowhere to hide one."

"Thank you," he said and realized he had clenched his fists in an attempt to stop his hands from shaking.

He always had to hide any sign of weakness, even when he didn't need to. It was in his blood.

He trusted Dominique completely.

She would never use any weakness against him.

She didn't play games.

At least none like that.

She smiled. "Does she know about me?" she asked. "Your daughter. Does she know about me?"

"She knows that there's someone special, but we agreed..."

She waved him away. "It doesn't matter. I just thought it might be easier if I was able to tell her who I was, she would trust me."

"She's smart. She'll get it. Just help the rest of us get inside. That's all I ask."

Dominique smiled again and, in that moment, Danjuma knew she wasn't going to be content with just opening a gate if she could do more.

"There's one more thing," he said, trying to think how to say what he had to say without losing his shit. He chose to keep it simple. "There might be other young girls in there."

"Others?"

He nodded. "I think the guy running the show, the Boss, is wrapped up in sex trafficking. Children."

She said nothing, but the horror in her eyes spoke volumes.

"Is that why Lori was taken?"

He shook his head. He told her about Dana, the missing boyfriend, the trip to the tiny apartment and their dumb plan to catch the cheater. Everything. He didn't hold back anything; he couldn't, even if he had wanted to. He felt weak and vulnerable, but he trusted her to see this side of him. Her, and no one else. The minute he walked back out of the door that vulnerability would be gone, replaced by the steel mask he wore for the world.

"The problem is they could ship her out of that place with the others."

"You've got eyes on the compound?" she asked.

He nodded.

"And there's no chance the girls have already gone?"

He shook his head again. His answer was born out of hope rather than any sort of certainty. She could well have been smuggled out of there, he just had to hope not, and he wasn't one to let his life revolve around hope.

"We'll find her," Dominique promised. "And we'll get any other girls out that we can."

Danjuma nodded.

There was much left to do, plans to put in place, but he didn't want to leave. He didn't want to leave her.

It was Dominique who made the first move to leave.

"I need to sort a few things," she said. "Text me the name and address of the garage and let me know when I can have it to myself."

She touched his knee, almost the first contact since they had been together in the apartment and got to her feet.

"It'll be alright," she promised. A promise she couldn't know if she could keep.

She gave him the lightest of kisses on his cheek and was gone.

He would owe her. They all would.

Sol Danjuma wasn't a man accustomed to being in debt.

CHAPTER
TWENTY-SIX

Boss had doubled the watch.

Daudi was on the wall again.

It was the first time since Lebna's body had been dumped at his feet.

It felt strange to be back.

The word was he was pulling night-watch for the next week as punishment for fucking up. He knew he'd fucked up. And so did everyone else. They also knew he was the reason none of them were allowed to go into Freetown.

But night watch meant he only had to take abuse from three of the other guys, not the entire compound.

"You see anything out there, Shithead?" One of the others asked. "Like a speeding fucking car?" In the semi-darkness he could barely make out who it was. He didn't really care. It was cold. He wanted something hot or something strong. Either would do.

"Nothing," he said.

It was a clear night. Anything approaching down the long road would have been visible from a mile away, even in the dark.

He saw something move in a shadow but dismissed it. The shape was no bigger than a small dog and there were plenty of those roaming the planes. In the daytime, they'd have taken pot shots at it for fun, but not at night. Gunshots at night meant something different.

He took a turn across the length of the wall. The idea was to keep moving to keep warm. It was then that he realized he was the only one on the walk. In the courtyard below him, a brazier burned. The other three guards were all huddled around it, their hands wrapped around hot drinks.

"Is there one of those down there for me?" he called down.

The three men looked up at him. One laughed. "You can get your own if one of us comes up to relieve you later."

He nodded, even though they wouldn't be able to see it, and carried on pacing. Bastards one and all.

Every now and then he stopped and turned, retracing his steps along the wall, and glanced down to see if there were any signs of life, either outside or inside the compound. None of his supposed watch mates showed any inclination to relieve him so he could warm himself by the fire.

When he reached the far end of the walkway this time, he was sure he saw something, but only for a moment, then it was gone, and he was left doubting himself.

He knew that he should tell the others but didn't want to face their ridicule if he was wrong. He wasn't used to doubting himself. Daudi remained motionless, staring at the same spot in the dark night, letting his eyes adjust as he sought the source of what he was sure had been an all-too brief glow in the darkness.

When he was finally sure he'd been wrong, he saw it again.

"You three," he rasped, not taking his eye off the spot. He refused to even blink in case he lost the mark in the dark. "There's something out there!"

"What the fuck are you whimpering about?" one of the others said.

"There's something out there," he repeated, resisting the impulse to point, lest who or whatever was out there saw.

More than a little reluctantly, one of the fire-watchers finally moved away from the brazier and climbed the ladder to join him on the wall.

"Where?" he demanded.

This time Daudi pointed, but there was nothing to be seen.

"Should we go out and take a look?" Daudi asked.

"At what? There's nothing there. Just how fucking stupid are you? Stay, watch, and if you see it again, signal us. Otherwise shut the fuck up."

"But..." he started to protest but was cut off before he could voice his complaint.

"Yeah, yeah, I know, you haven't had a break, you haven't had the chance to get warm. You're tired and you're thirsty. I'll send a mug up for you, OK? Now stop whining and do your job."

The man left him on the wall.

"Fucker," Daudi hissed under his breath. A moment later he heard the chatter of voices below, swiftly followed by laughter. "Fuckers," he said, louder this time, and maybe they could hear him. He didn't care.

A little later a mug of coffee was brought up to him, followed by another chuckle of laughter. They'd probably pissed or spat in it. Daudi was past caring. He wrapped his hands around the mug and held it close to his face to draw whatever warmth he could from it.

For the next couple of hours, he walked the wall, stopping and staring in the same direction every time without seeing the light again.

By the time the sky began to brighten to the sun, with dawn threatening to break, he was willing to admit he had imagined it.

A clatter of boots coming up the ladder announced the end of his watch.

A quick glance down showed that the three men who'd supposedly shared the night watch with him had already gone.

"All quiet?" asked the first man up the ladder.

Daudi considered the question for a moment, deciding he'd had enough ridicule for one night. "Nothing worth mentioning," he said.

It would be a couple of hours before the rest of the camp began to stir. If he was going to grab some sleep it was likely to be now or never.

CHAPTER
TWENTY-SEVEN

Connors was getting twitchy.

He'd tried to leave the room a couple of times, but each time someone had been waiting to politely ask him to go back inside and wait. And polite as it was, it was unnerving. He felt caged. Which of course he was. The fourth time wasn't a charm.

The door was locked.

That was when he started to freak out.

Why the fuck would they lock him up?

He tried the windows.

They had a lock on them that ensured they could only open a few inches; barely enough to let air in. Even if he had been able to open them all the way, looking down he realized that he was on the fourth floor, and it was a long way down.

Nope, he was a prisoner, in the most comfortable cell he could imagine, with high-end en-suite bathroom that put the hotel where he'd been staying to shame, but a prisoner just the same.

Trays of food and drink were brought to him by a mountain of a man. Staring at the window, all he could think was, even if he escaped this prison where the hell would he go?

When the sun started its cooling descent Danjuma came to see him. It was the first time he'd seen the drug lord since he'd been sent to the room.

He couldn't help himself, part of him was relieved at the sight of the man, part felt pure dread, but it came out like an enraged, "What the fuck's happening? And why the fuck have you locked me in here?"

"For your own protection," Danjuma said, smoothly.

He was calm and that calmness only served to project an air of menace, with Danjuma forming a solid barrier between Connors and the door.

"What's that supposed to mean? Protect me from who?" The unspoken question, *who is going to try to hurt me while I'm here?*

"You may not want to believe me, but it really is for your own good. You go out there, you overhear something, something about my business, you get some dumbass notion to try and use it as leverage and I have to kill you, because there's no way I can let you walk out of here knowing anything that might undermine my authority or operation, you understand?"

"You wouldn't…"

"Of course I would. Just remember you're the one who came to me for help, not the other way around. If you want help, you'll keep on being fucking patient, but if you don't, then great, I'll get someone to drop you back at that shithole we picked you up from and you can sort your own problems. You're welcome to go at any point. Just say the word."

"Sorry, sorry... I appreciate it, I know you don't have to help me..." Connors said, suddenly humbled. He looked away, breaking eye contact. "Is there any news?"

"Pertaining to your mess, no, not yet, and in the spirit of honesty we've developed here, I've had other things to deal with. With luck there will be news tomorrow. I suggest you watch some TV, get an early night, and try not to think. But if you only do one thing, make sure it's taking a shower. You are an olfactory nightmare, man."

Danjuma left him, locking the door again. That tumbler dropping into place sounded menacing.

Connors sank down on the edge of the bed, lost for words.

He couldn't remember ever feeling so powerless.

A couple of days ago he'd been on top of the world; everything had been coming up roses, and now he was at the bottom of the shit heap, not even getting to nourish those roses while he waited for someone else to dig him out.

He lifted his arm and sniffed. Danjuma was right. He smelled like shit.

CHAPTER
TWENTY-EIGHT

It had taken Dominique longer than she'd expected, but she'd managed to grab a few hours' sleep before her alarm woke her.

She was ready to leave long before the call from Danjuma came.

"Everything set?"

"Good to go," she assured him. "The car is still in the garage; we just need to pick it up."

"Perfect. I'll pick you up," he told her. "Be ready in thirty minutes."

It wasn't a question.

She wasn't about to wait for him in the street; that invited situations she had no intention of getting herself into. The dress was the tightest she had in her closet, bought for the color, and the fact it made her look like a hooker. Sometimes the fantasy was the best part of the seduction after all. She couldn't wear anything underneath; nothing could hide under that, especially not a weapon.

It was all about keeping eyes on her rather than the car.

She was still adjusting the second skin of her dress when the horn sounded outside.

She was already out of the vehicle and leaning against it, waving a hand when he saw her watching him. She grabbed the bag she'd packed with a clean change of clothes and a few pieces she'd picked out of the laundry basket.

"Not that I don't appreciate it, but what's with the dress?" Danjuma asked when they were both in the car and he had pulled into what little traffic was on the road.

She explained her thinking.

He nodded like a wise old owl.

"Good thinking," he said.

"So, where's the mark who's getting me inside?"

"At the club. We'll pick him up before we get the car."

"The club?"

"There's a nice little room in the cellar... quite accommodating."

"Ah," she said.

Dominique knew exactly what kind of life Danjuma led, and the kind of business he was involved in, but she didn't need to know the details. It was better if she didn't know.

They had a reciprocal arrangement; he knew that she had secrets of her own and gave her the same space.

He would no more ask about her past, than she would ask about his.

He'd guessed wrongly about the scars and there had been no need to correct him. There had been hints, of course, things that had seeped into conversation without her meaning for them to. It was hard to lie all the time about who you had been, and it was enough for him to realize what kind of things she'd done in her former life.

When she'd come here it had only ever been as a short-term stay, a pause to give herself some headspace, and exorcise some of those demons that haunted her. But she liked it here. And then she found Danjuma. They were good for each other; he had saved her whether he knew it or not. She never asked anything from him, and this was the first time he'd asked her for something.

"What state is he in?"

"A little bruised," Danjuma said. "Nothing broken."

"Good, not too bruised, I hope. We don't need the complications."

"Nothing beyond an unhappy boyfriend," he said, lips twitching into the parody of a smile.

"Or my pimp," she said, reading between the unspoken lines. "I'm guessing that's what you were thinking?"

"Perhaps, but I'd never say it, even in that dress."

"Like I said," Dominique said. "I was saving it for the right occasion."

"Pimp it is then. Our American friend thinks he's rescuing you, taking you to a better life."

"That works."

She was about to ask more when Danjuma's phone rang.

"I'd better take this," he said, answering the call on the car's hands-free system.

"Danjuma," he said.

"We'll be heading back into town when the next pair arrive," the voice said.

"Anything to report?"

"Nothing that can't wait."

"Come straight to the club, you can fill me in."

Danjuma ended the call and drove on for a little while in silence. There was clearly something on his mind. Whatever it was, he would tell her if he wanted to, no amount of pushing would change that. She assumed he was thinking about his daughter. She hoped that call had confirmed she was still in that place, and that she was safe.

"She'll be fine," Dominique said.

"I know," Danjuma said, but she was sure that his smile was forced.

He shifted gear, leaving his hand on the stick.

She placed her own on top and squeezed to reassure him.

She hoped it would be enough until this was all over.

———

Dominique had only been to the club on a couple of occasions, both of them before she and Danjuma had become whatever this thing was that they had become. They had agreed early on that they would keep what they had between themselves. She knew about the girls, of course and they knew that there was someone in his life. There had been moments she'd wished that things could be different, but those soon passed. She wasn't one for sentimentality. Things were about to change though; she knew it would be hard to keep herself out of his life after this. She'd be out of the box and it would be impossible to put her back in. She didn't know if that was a good or bad thing.

The door to the club was closed, but not locked.

Danjuma led the way inside.

It smelled different to any club she'd been in, but then she'd seldom been to one the morning after people had been partying through the night. The lights were bright, exposing the wear and tear. The tables were clear. She heard the sound of a vacuum cleaner, but the bar was covered with empty bottles and dirty glasses. Behind it, a man sorted through them, tossing the bottles into a large plastic bin. The glasses he loaded into a dishwasher. It was going to take most of the day to get through them all.

Danjuma exchanged nods with the man, not breaking his stride.

They descended.

Outside the door at the far end of the cellar, a man sat on a wooden chair, tipped back on two legs, rocking backwards and forwards. His eyes were closed but it was obvious he wasn't asleep.

"You been here all night, Rakeem?" Danjuma asked.

The man dropped the chair onto all four legs and opened his eyes.

"I went upstairs and grabbed a few hours' sleep on one of the sofas. But I left one of the other guys down here, just in case. The door hasn't been opened since you locked it." All the time he was saying this he hadn't taken his eyes off Dominique. "Who's this?" he asked eventually, a shark-like grin spreading across his face.

"Our secret weapon," Danjuma said. "Let's get the door open, shall we?"

Rakeem got to his feet.

The key was already in the lock. Danjuma could have turned it himself, but Dominique recognized the power play. Danjuma was in charge, and he was showing it. What she wasn't sure of for a moment was whose benefit it was for; hers or Rakeem's.

The moment the door opened, and the foul odor of the room hit them, he nodded for the other man to take care of the bucket that stood in the corner. Rakeem scurried inside, grabbed it, and holding it at arm's length gave Dominique the briefest of glances before he left to empty the shit.

The man inside the room lay curled up on a camp bed. A chair had been pushed against the opposite wall. There were a couple of severed cable ties on the floor. It didn't take much in the way of fantasy to imagine what it had looked like in here last night. It wasn't the first time she had seen a room like this, with that unique mixture of sweat, piss, fear and worse.

The man's face was a mess.

She wasn't sure how much of the bruising and cuts would disappear when he'd had the chance to freshen up, some, sure, but far from all. They were going to need to rehearse the story about him being beaten up by her pimp.

"Has he had anything to eat?" she asked, as if the man couldn't understand a word she said. He pushed a plate with his toe, offering up a plate with a few crumbs on it as proof that he understood all well and good.

There were a couple of empty plastic water bottles under the bed.

"Okay, we need to get him cleaned up," she told Danjuma. "I assume you have a change of clothes for him?"

Danjuma nodded. "There's a bag with his stuff, it was in the car when we picked him up."

"Anything else?"

"Apart from the consignment of drugs he stole, you mean?" he laughed.

"Yes, apart from the drugs."

"No weapon, if that's what you're asking."

"What happened to it then?"

"How do you mean?"

"He came to a meeting with you as the hired muscle and didn't have a gun on him? I don't buy it."

"He would have had it taken off him long before he got anywhere near me."

"That's not the point, Sol. He would still have brought one to the party. People like him always do. So where is it?"

"I'll ask Rakeem when he gets back, but does it matter?"

"Maybe not, but if he didn't have one, then he's a complete amateur and I like to know what I'm working with," Dominique reasoned.

The man on the bed looked up. He spoke for the first time since they had arrived. "They took it from me, the two guys who picked me up, the ones who thought it would be fun to kick the shit out of me before they put me in the trunk of the car." He had the voice of a man who was broken; a man who thought he might have nothing left to lose but he had been offered a lifeline.

She pitied him.

"Give it back to him," she said.

"Are you crazy?"

The man on the bed clearly couldn't believe what he was hearing either.

"We're selling an illusion here. He needs a piece. No bullets, though," she added. "The people we're going to see will *expect* him to come packing. You boys like your guns. If he doesn't have one, it'll look wrong, and even if they don't see it straight away, it'll set an instinctive mistrust going."

"And if they see it's empty?"

"We say he emptied it into my pimp and left his corpse back in Freetown. But we don't volunteer the information."

"Sounds like you've done this kind of thing before," the man said.

"Enough to know how not to get myself killed. Let's get you cleaned up, shall we? And maybe we can all grab some breakfast and get our stories straight?" She looked from one man to the other to get their agreement and they nodded in turn.

CHAPTER
TWENTY-NINE

Forty minutes later they were sitting in Danjuma's office.

Rakeem wasn't happy about being treated like a servant, but he'd gone out to pick up breakfast for the four of them. There was something about the man that Dominique didn't quite trust, but she couldn't say exactly what.

There was certainly something going on between him and Danjuma.

Travis on the other hand just seemed grateful to be out of the room and not being punched. He drank several cups of strong black coffee and cleared his plate before Dominique had eaten even half of hers. The man looked more alive than he had before, having cleaned himself up, shaved, and put on a change of clothes. But there were still several bruises on his face and the scabs of a couple of cuts, one above the eye, one to his fat lip. Even so, he looked much better.

The way that he got in and out of a chair though, suggested that his body had taken a beating that would be slower in healing.

"What do you need me to do?" he asked. His question was addressed to Danjuma, but it was Dominique who answered.

"Nothing," she said. "At least nothing more than get us inside. You don't need to be a great actor. We will have the consignment with us, it's business as usual."

They'd spun a story about needing him to get her inside so Dominique could take a look at what was going on in the old army base. There was no benefit in telling him more than that; the more he knew, the more likely it was he would screw up.

"What's to say this prick won't just throw you to the wolves once he thinks he's safe?" Rakeem asked. He got a sharp look from Danjuma.

The American looked up from his coffee. "Because if I do that, I'll be the one at fault. I'll be the one who lied to them to get her in there. Best case, they'll kill both of us and keep the drugs. That's why. And frankly, I'm not sure what's stopping you from killing me when I come out."

"You're smarter than you look," Danjuma said. "Unlike your partner."

"What are you going to do with him?"

"I haven't decided. Do you have any special requests?"

"Naw, I don't have anything against him. He's going to be in enough shit as it is." Travis said, a sudden spark of fire in his eyes before he shook his head.

"Feeling guilty?"

"I've got nothing to feel guilty about. He was planning to do the same to me. I just got my retaliation in early. When the goods were on the boat that would be it. I would be surplus to requirements."

"Whatever happened to honor amongst thieves," Danjuma laughed.

"You come here acing like the big white man," Rakeem grunted, "Come to teach the poor black men a thing or two about this bad world, like we don't know shit."

Danjuma slapped a palm on the table, rattling cutlery on plates and splashing coffee onto the wood. "That's enough," he said. "It's neither the time nor the place for a lecture on equality. We give our *friend* here the drugs, he takes them and Dominique into that place. He gets to do his deal and drives away with the cash, and that's the end of his part in the story. That's not what this is all about. We get my little girl back or I kill every last mutha-fuckah in that place."

"My passport?" Travis asked, not sure if he was pushing his luck in asking for it, but knowing he needed it to sell the illusion and drive away with the cash.

Danjuma opened the drawer of his desk and pulled out two US passports, opened the first to check the photograph, then dropped it back in the drawer. He examined the second one before sliding it across his desk. "Here you go," he said.

They were interrupted by the arrival of two men who looked like they hadn't slept. Dominique guessed they were the men Danjuma had spoken to in the car. There were no more chairs in the office, but they were happy to stand.

Danjuma nodded to them in greeting. "Everything okay?"

The two men looked at the American and frowned before Danjuma said, "It's okay, you can talk in front of him."

"All quiet," one of them said. "No vehicles in or out."

"Lookouts?"

"Four to start with but it soon went down to one."

"Sloppy," Domonique said.

"The others were out of sight. He kept looking down inside the compound."

"Did he see you?"

There was a moment of hesitation, followed by a moment of truth. "Almost. But we were too far away for anyone to have been able to see us properly. It was dark."

"What aren't you telling me?"

The two new arrivals looked at each other, as if deciding which of them should speak. "He kept looking in our direction, staring at us, but he couldn't have seen us."

"Which one of you got out of the car?" Dominique asked, refusing to believe that they might be as stupid as she feared.

"We both did," one of them said, but we'd turned off the overhead light, we ain't stupid."

Danjuma nodded but Dominque wasn't satisfied.

Something had drawn the lookout's attention.

"Must have been a long cold night," she said. "Especially when you couldn't turn on the engine to get warm. Bet you got through a packet of cigarettes."

"We only had half a packet between us," one of them said. "We had to make them last."

And then the penny dropped. She knew exactly what the lookout had seen. So did Danjuma.

"You stupid fucks."

CHAPTER
THIRTY

Boss had reached a decision.

It hadn't been an easy one, but it needed to be made.

The girl those two idiots had brought here was a headache, and potentially so much more. He didn't want her being here screwing up the deal he'd invested so much in. Not now that it was coming together.

Her situation needed to be sorted and sorted quickly.

In the end it came down to expedience and opportunity; the other girls they were holding would be moving on tomorrow. The simplest solution was to send her with them, even if she was a little older than the rest. That didn't matter in the grand scheme of things. He'd throw in a sweetener; an extra girl without asking for more money. His partners down the supply line were business-people, they'd appreciate the added profitability on the deal. He could have pushed for extra on the deal, and get it, but it paid to be beneficent.

When he asked one of the guards to fetch the idiot for him there was no question about who he meant.

Daudi.

He would forever be the idiot.

At least until he was worm food.

When Daudi finally appeared in front of him, looking sheepish and like shit, Boos almost pitied him. Almost. Night watch was a bastard at the best of times. He'd had maybe two hours sleep, assuming he'd fallen asleep as soon as his head hit the pillow.

"You wanted to see me, Boss?"

"The girl, you know where she is at the moment?"

Daudi shook his head. "Last I knew she was in the canteen, being grilled."

Boss nodded. "She's been moved to one of the storage rooms behind the kitchen," he said. It was one of the few places with a working lock on it and had the benefit of the old fortress's defenses, barred windows. It functioned well as a holding cell. He didn't want to waste a man keeping an eye on her and couldn't risk her wandering around. "I've decided what we're going to do with her."

Daudi waited, not moving a muscle. He was waiting for the kill order, Boss realized, knowing it would be his responsibility because he was the dumb fuck who'd brought her here. Boss let him sweat it a moment more before he said, "I'm sending her off with the other girls tomorrow."

"You can't do that."

Silence.

Boss stared at the other man, his rage rising.

"You did this, Daudi. It is on you. We can't let her go. If we do, she brings a warlord's wrath to our door looking for retribution. We could have stayed at home and died there if that was what we were looking for. The alternative is to kill her and bury the girl in the desert. Are you volunteering?"

"No," Daudi said, visibly shaking.

"Then she goes on the truck with the others," Danjuma said. "There is no viable alternative.

"Why are you telling me this?"

"Ah, finally a better question. Because," Danjuma said, drawing the agony out slowly, "you'll be going with them."

"What?"

"I need someone to ride along, be my eyes and ears on the deal, and lucky you, you were the first name on my lips."

"But..."

"Think of it this way, the good news is you won't be on watch tonight, you'll need to be fresh in the morning, so you get to rest up." Daudi nodded, knowing resistance was futile. "Now though, go see that she's fed and put her in with the other girls. From now on, she isn't anything special. Understood?"

Daudi said nothing, but he didn't move, either.

"Problem?" Boss asked, knowing what the answer would be if there was one. It had a number of bullets in his desk drawer.

Daudi shook his head.

"No, Boss," he said, then left the room.

As he left Boss knew that he was making the right decision.

The boy was fast becoming a liability.

Better to kill two problems with one stone...

CHAPTER
THIRTY-ONE

The key was in the lock.

Daudi hesitated before he turned it.

"She's been hollering for hours," one of the guys from the kitchen said. "The bitch just won't shut up, screaming and shouting and just raging like she's trying to raise the fucking dead in there. I don't know how she hasn't screamed herself hoarse."

"Has she had any breakfast?"

The man shrugged, "Don't know, don't really care."

"Make something for her," Daudi told him.

The man shrugged, not about to argue because he didn't know where the order was coming from. "Give me a minute."

He'd left him standing by the door. He couldn't help but wonder about the room's history; what needed to be kept safe on an army base, next to the kitchen? You wouldn't store weapons or ammunition. And then it hit him, the logical answer: alcohol. The soldiers needed rations to keep them in line, but not free access to the liquor, because they couldn't be trusted.

"Here you go," the man said, returning a few minutes later with a plate of bacon, beans, fried potatoes, and a thick slice of bread.

Daudi hesitated, seeing the knife and fork, but the man read his mind. "She'll be lucky to cut through the bacon with it," he said, laughing.

"Let me open the door first," Daudi said as the man held the plate out for him.

The girl was a ball of fury. She charged at the door even before it had finished swinging open.

Daudi barely reacted in time, arms out to defend himself from her wildly thrashing hands with nails as she clawed at his flesh. He managed to wrap his arms around her, holding her tight until she finally stopped struggling.

All the while, the man holding the plate of food stood laughing at him.

"Enough!" Daudi said, refusing to relinquish his hold until she was spent. "This isn't going to get you anywhere. You need to know something, girl, even if you get past me, there are a hundred others out there bigger and stronger—and nastier—than me. Where do you think you are going to go?"

He relaxed his grip and she stepped back. He was anything but relaxed, though, ready for a fresh onslaught from the girl.

It didn't come.

"Why have I been locked up in here all night?" she demanded, still spitting rage and pent-up frustration. "When my father hears about this..."

"It was for your own benefit," Daudi told her, not sure she'd believe him anyway, but figuring right now truth was the best policy between them if he had any chance of building a bond that would see them safely out of this. "If you'd gone outside in the dark, we couldn't have guaranteed your safety."

"There aren't any wild animals out there, especially not inside these damned walls."

"Oh, there are, especially within these walls," he said. "There are worse things here than out in the desert, girl, believe me. I live amongst them. Now eat before it gets cold."

She glanced at the plate with an obvious look of disgust. It fell a long way short of her usual spoiled breakfast. She was a child of privilege. Hers was a different life to anyone living in the compound. But food was food, and without it she'd starve. He didn't want her being weak on their journey; that would present a host of different problems for him to deal with.

"It's this or nothing," he said. "And it could be a long time before you get another chance to eat."

"What? Are you planning on starving me? Is that it, some kind of sick punishment?"

Daudi shrugged. "Hardly. But life has a way of turning on us, so I figure it's best to make the most of it while you can. Why don't you come through, you can eat it at the table?"

"Have you eaten?" she asked.

"Not yet," he said. "It was my turn for night watch, so I've been at the walls all night."

"I'll bring another plate out," the other man said. "But if she causes trouble, it's on you."

"I'll live with it," Daudi assured him.

There was no one else in the canteen. The girl glanced in the direction of the door to the outside world but made no move towards it. The rage she'd shown when he'd opened the door was spent. She slumped into a chair at one of the tables. Daudi put the plate down in front of her.

"You seriously expect me to eat this?" she said, moving food around the plate with her fork.

"It's that or starve," he said. "It's not like you're being asked to split a rat open with your fingernails and pull off strips of raw meat. It's good food. You want something to drink? Water? Milk?"

"Coffee," she said. "Black and strong."

Daudi nodded to the guy from the kitchen. "Make that two, will you?"

The girl pushed the food around a little more, a look of disgust on her face. Daudi said nothing. He'd done everything he could to get her to eat, bar force it down her throat.

She still hadn't tasted a bite before a plate arrived for him, along with the two mugs of coffee.

She added three spoons of sugar to the heavy black liquid, tasted it, then added another.

"I like it sweet," she said after she had stirred it a seemingly endless number of times.

Daudi scooped up a forkful of beans.

Eventually she did the same.

"What's going to happen to me?" She asked. Again, it crossed his mind to lie, to put her at her ease with the promise that they'd let her go, but that would be proved a lie in no time at all, and undermine any sort of fledgling relationship, instead he said something close to the truth.

"You'll be heading out of here with a bunch of girls and given work to do."

She said nothing.

She took another mouthful of beans.

The reality of the situation was sinking in. He tried to think how his own mind would be working in her place. She'd be thinking about biding her time, knowing there was going to be one moment somewhere along the chain of coming events where she could try to make her escape.

One moment.

It was down to him to make sure she didn't take advantage of it if he wanted to buy his way back into Boss's good graces. Or make sure that she did, if he wanted to trade his way into a different life of servitude with her father. If that was even an option.

"I'll take you to join the other girls when you're done eating," he said.

CHAPTER
THIRTY-TWO

They had to wait until late afternoon before they set off.

Domonique wanted to make sure that they arrived late enough for the question of staying the night to seem natural. Travis had assured her that was the arrangement, but she didn't intend to take any chances. Get there too soon, and maybe this Boss character would hurry them out of there before the sun went down.

For her plan to stand any hope of working, she had to be in the compound overnight.

Those extra hours would give Danjuma the time to get his men in place.

Then it was just down to her to fulfill her side of the bargain.

The car drove well enough for its age and handled the rutted road as well as could be hoped. Travis had wanted to drive, but with his bruises it was pretty obvious it would hurt him unnecessarily, so she saved him the suffering She'd fitted their ride with a few surprises that would be essential if her plan was going to work.

As far as Travis was concerned this was a fact-finding mission; that Danjuma just wanted to know what was going on inside those walls. The other man had no idea if his daughter was in there. Dominique would have preferred it if he hadn't even known there was a chance that she was, but someone had let it slip. Her guess? Rakeem. She'd come across men like him before, men who did things grudgingly, but always with their own interests first.

She had thought to ask Danjuma about him, but it wasn't her place to question his choice of lieutenants. Anything more than basic help was risking a dynamic shift in their relationship, and she wasn't sure the man was ready for that, or even the appearance of it.

"So, how come you got saddled with babysitting me?" Travis asked. "I assume Danjuma has got something on you?"

She laughed at the unintended double entendre. "Something like that," she said.

"So, what happens if I kill you before we get there?" She looked at him, no words exchanged. "I mean, what if I take the car and the drugs and just drive like the fucking devil is on my heels?"

This time there were no laughs. "First, what makes you think you could kill me? I think you should consider yourself lucky that you're still alive. I'd rather not have to give you a demonstration, but trust me," she said. "You'd be out cold before you laid a hand on me. Then I'd think long and hard about if it was worth keeping you alive."

She didn't know if she'd unwittingly contributed to his newfound bravado but the way he reached out to grab the handbrake was almost enough to catch her by surprise. Almost. The car slewed to one side violently. She fought to control it, but in a single moment her right hand shot from the steering wheel and swung into the side of the man's head with blinding force. It was instinct. Training. She wished he hadn't made her do it. His cries were wretched. In pain, he released his grip on the lever. Dominque didn't spare so much as a side-eye to see what sort of state he was in. She focused on maintaining control of the car with one hand, and releasing the brake with the other.

"Next time I won't be so gentle," she promised him. "Do we understand each other now?"

She glanced across to see him nod, even though it was clearly uncomfortable to do so. He wasn't going to try anything for a while.

"You're lucky," she said.

"Lucky? How the fuck am I lucky?"

"I was aiming for your Adam's apple."

He fell silent, but his hands remained on his ear for a while, wincing every time the car caught a pothole.

"How far do you think you'd get if you managed to get away? Seriously, say I just gave you the car and waved you off?"

"Far enough," he said. "I could be over the border before anyone even realized that I was making a run for it."

"Fucking hell you are a fool. Are all Americans this dense? I fitted a tracker to this pile of shit last night so Danjuma can see *exactly* where it is. There are already men positioned along the road keeping watch. If I let you go, you'd be dead long before you reached the border."

"But he needs me. Without me, he'll never get inside that place."

"He doesn't need you. He needs a white man. There's nothing stopping him from sending your former partner, Connors, in there. You've already told us everything we need to know to get inside. No, believe me when I tell you this, you are only here because of the color of your skin."

"Connors? You really think you could trust that piece of shit to do anything?"

"I don't trust him any more than I trust you," she said. "But you have one thing going for you that he doesn't, right now. I know that you won't be stupid enough to do anything once we get inside the old fortress. And I know you won't because it'll see you dead just as quickly as if you pulled the trigger yourself." He didn't argue with anything she said. "And if Danjuma decided that he'd rather have Connors here instead of you, he'd put the gun to your head and pull the trigger himself." Even as she said it, she realized that it was true. It wasn't something she had given a moment's thought to before. He wouldn't give an order for someone to do something he wasn't prepared to do himself. If he'd thought he would have been able to drive through the gates himself, he'd be behind the wheel now.

They passed a car parked up at the side of the road. It was beside a stand of naked trees. The two men inside glanced across at her as she drove past them. One nodded. Danjuma had told her they would be there. They were a reassuring sight. He was good for his word. Travis gave them the briefest of glances before staring straight ahead again. He removed his hand from his ear, which still burned red raw.

Less than half a mile later they reached the turning off the road.

"This is it then," she said, barely slowing as she took the turn.

The track was in worse condition than she'd hoped but no worse than she'd expected. She took more care to avoid the gaping potholes than she needed to. She didn't want anything shaking loose before they reached their destination, making progress painfully slow.

The last time she'd driven like this she was being shot at. This was an improvement on that, at least.

Ahead of them the walled fortress grew larger and more imposing as they approached.

Dominique made a couple of men, both with rifles held low, standing on the wall, watching her approach.

She drove on, interminably slowly, not wanting to spook them.

After what seemed like forever, she pulled the car to a halt just outside the gates and killed the engine.

She waited, praying Travis was not about to screw things up and get them both killed. The problem was she'd long since stopped believing in any sort of god that might have been listening.

CHAPTER
THIRTY-THREE

"They've just gone inside," the man on the other end of the call said, confirming that everything was moving forward according to plan. With so many moving pieces in play it was hard to feel good about it, even with Dominique running the show out there. There was still too much room for things to go to shit, and fast. All it took was one idiot to panic, or one smart guy to see through her. He felt helpless and he didn't like the feeling one little bit.

Danjuma hung up without comment.

Dana paced the living room of their family home, barely keeping her agitation in check.

"Why aren't you out there doing something?" she asked.

It was the same question he'd asked himself a hundred times that day already. He told her what he told himself. "What do you think I could do that isn't already being done?"

He'd already gone through the plan with his daughter. He knew her arguments, they were his, too, or at least that part of him that felt utterly helpless. The longer Lori was inside that place, the more danger she was in. It was a fairly simple equation. But they had no choice but to wait. Darkness was their best asset. Try anything in daylight and there would be greater risk than just Lori. He wasn't prepared to risk any more lives than he was already doing, including Dominique's.

"This woman, the one you sent in there," Dana said eventually, reasoning it through. "It's her, isn't it?"

"That depends on who you mean by her?"

"Don't play games, Dad. It's the woman you're sleeping with. No one else would do this for you. Do you love her?"

He said nothing, not sure how much he could tell her when he wasn't really sure himself.

"You're not denying it then?" she said, breaking the silence. "How could you?"

That hit him hard. "How could I what? Betray your mother? She's been dead for a long time, girl."

"Don't be an idiot, dad," she bit back. "Not that. You deserve to be happy, and if she does that for you then I'm glad."

"What then?" he asked.

"How could you put her in danger like this? After mum... after everything..."

"Because it's the only way to get your sister back. Besides, I trust Domonique. She's more than capable of looking after herself."

"Dominique?" She gave a slight smile at the name. "Why have you tried to keep her from us? I mean, you never even mention her..."

"Because it's nothing to do with you," he said, a little more sharply than he had intended. "She's nothing to do with anyone else."

"Well, she is now," Dana concluded and that was hard to argue with.

He nodded in acceptance. Danjuma stared at his phone. There was no one left to call, and no one else that would call him. Unless something went wrong. Silence was golden. "I should go," he said.

"Go where?"

"To make sure that everyone knows what they have to do."

"What about me? What am I supposed to do in all of this?"

"Stay here," he said. "Make sure that idiot in the guest room gets fed and watered."

"What are you going to do with him?" she asked. And then, "Are you going to kill him?"

"Why would I do that? He's an idiot who is out of his depth, nothing more. It suits me to keep him out of his depth, for now at least. When this is all done, I'll send him on his way."

"Really? You won't hurt him?"

Danjuma shrugged. "He may be an idiot, but he has done me no harm. I don't hurt people for no reason."

"Then why not send him on his way now?"

Danjuma thought about it for a moment, seriously considering it, just because his little girl had asked. But the answer was always going to be no. "Because he asked for my help, and I can't spare the time to solve his problems while I'm trying to get your sister back. When she is home, I will honor my promise and help him."

"Then go and get her and bring Dominique back here so we can get to know our new mom properly," she grinned that wicked grin she'd inherited from her mother.

"You sure?"

She nodded. "If you can find Lebna, bring him back, too. I'm frightened for him."

Sol Danjuma pulled his eldest daughter close for a moment and planted a kiss on her cheek. "I'll do what I can," he promised, knowing that Lebna's welfare was far down his list of priorities. Not that he was about to admit that to her.

CHAPTER
THIRTY-FOUR

Boss watched the car pull in slowly through the defensive gates of the compound.

Several of his men pointed at it, like it was a unicorn or something.

The car had seen better days. He couldn't imagine it seeing many worse ones.

He motioned to one of the men to open the passenger side to let the man out.

"What the fuck happened to you?" he asked before he was even halfway out of the car; one foot on solid ground. "You look like shit." And then a second thought hit. "And you didn't say anything about bringing a woman with you. I don't like surprises."

"Let's say that the two things are related," Travis said, wincing as he bent down to look into the car. "You can get out now."

The minute that Dominique stepped out of the car, all eyes were on her. That was the way it was always going to be. She was not someone you could ignore, especially when she wriggled to pull her skimpy dress down over her covers. There was no modesty, it was a purely sexual move, meant to be watched. She knew exactly what she was doing.

"Well," laughed Boss, a lecherous smile spreading across his ugly face. "It looks as though it was a price worth paying." Boss motioned for two of his people to come forward, "You know what to do," he nodded towards Travis. "I'm not sure the lady needs searching, but it might be fun anyway."

"If anyone tries, they'll be searching for their cock for the next month," she said, with a smile that was all sweetness and light and utterly belied the words. She held her purse ready for inspection.

"You'll need to hand over any weapons, and your cell phones while you're here," Boss said. "Not that you'd get any reception out here. It's a dead zone. You can have them back when you leave."

Dominique nodded as she handed over her phone. It was a new burner she'd picked up and added a dozen numbers to, not that she thought they'd bother to check her call history. It was all about building the story. If they were *that* interested in checking her out, they'd be screwed anyway.

Travis handed his weapon without any resistance.

The man relieving him of it checked to see if it was loaded.

"It's empty," the man said, twisting his face in confusion as he looked at Boss.

"I used the last bullets as payback," Travis said without missing a beat.

"Let's get my shit done first," Boss chuckled. "Then we can help you reload before you leave. Wouldn't want you in the desert alone, unable to defend yourself."

The man who had taken Dominique's phone had slipped it into the pocket of his cargo pants as he went to the rear of the car to inspect the consignment they were carrying.

"In the trunk?" Boss asked.

"Inside the spare," Travis said.

The man popped the trunk and lifted out Dominique's bag. He unzipped it and rifled through the contents. "Hey, you fucking perv," she said. "Get your filthy hands out of my thong!"

There was a ripple of laughter from the men standing around, which had the immediate effect of lifting the mood.

The man zipped the backpack up and dumped it on the ground while he dealt with the spare. Dominique snatched it up. A couple of minutes later he had to the four bags of cocaine laid out on the closed trunk and Boss was laughing louder than any of the others.

He ushered them to follow him into one of the buildings.

Dominique scanned the surroundings, not enough to make it look like she was locking their positions and defenses in her mind. They saw a tourist or a whore, not a spy in their midst. She needed it to stay that way. The man led them into one of the buildings, through dank corridors, and into a room where a square safe sat against the wall behind an old metal desk that had seen better days. It was a relic of the fortress's past life.

The man who'd searched the car followed them inside. He placed the bags of white powder on the battered metal desk. "You need anything else, Boss?"

Boss shook his head. "Maybe our guests would like refreshments? A beer to celebrate?"

"Sounds good to me," Travis said. "Let's hope this is the beginning of a beautiful friendship."

"I don't have friends. I have associates, but if you can do this again, I can make an exception," Boss cracked a grin. "How soon can you get another consignment to me?"

"Four weeks, maybe."

Dominique didn't even look at him. The man was winging it, but at least he wasn't saying anything stupid like tomorrow. Deals this size needed time to be brokered. Channels needed to be opened, lines secured. She could have done it in a week, even without Danjuma, but she wasn't about to contradict him.

"Same amount? Same price?"

Travis gave the impression he was weighing up asking for more, then deciding upon friendship with his, "I don't see why not."

"A good deal for both of us then. It pays not to be greedy." The man turned on a swivel office chair that squealed its complaints as he produced a key for the safe.

There were stacks of money bundled up inside. He pulled several out in payment, there was a lot more in there, though. "You'll stay with us tonight? Accept our hospitality. Or would you rather return to Freetown," a lascivious smile cracked across his features as he suggested, "and find a hotel room for you and your... friend?"

"We'd better not," Dominique said, a side-eye glance to Travis. "There are people who might be looking for us."

That was enough for Boss. He smiled again. "In that case, my dear, you are most welcome here in our humble home. I will have a room made up for you," he shrugged an apology to Travis, "Sadly we do not have double beds. Only cheap mattresses, and bunks, but they are better than sleeping in the dirt." He waved his arms expansively. "This is not exactly Trump Towers. Think of it as a fun adventure at the beginning of your grand romance. You'll eat with us, of course."

"Of course," said Travis who mimicked Dominique's side-eye glance. "That OK with you, honey?"

"Sure. I'd like the chance to freshen up, though. Get the dusty roads off my skin."

"Of course," Boss said, as three bottles of beer were brought and placed on the desk where the coke had been moments before. "There'll be plenty of time for that."

He raised his bottle in salute as Dominique accepted hers.

The beer tasted warm, but she drank it down like it was the best stuff of her life.

CHAPTER
THIRTY-FIVE

The club was rammed.

All the lights were on and there was no music playing.

Outside, a sign told the world the place was closed. Muscle stood on the door, only letting the right people in. Danjuma looked around and saw a lot of familiar faces, some of whom worked for him, others were old friends he'd asked to lend a hand, despite knowing the risks involved if they offered it. To a man, they were all fiercely loyal to Danjuma. And now they knew about his missing daughter.

When Danjuma stood up, the dancehall fell silent.

"You know why you're here," he began. "It's been explained to you. I am not about to pluck heartstrings or make rash promises to you, but I want you to know that I appreciate each and every one of you in this room and the fact you have answered the call during my time of need. It will not be forgotten."

He ran through the plan, repeating the same things he'd said to most of them on the phone when he'd put out the call. There were others here he hadn't spoken to. Rakeem had been in contact with them. These were street warriors. They didn't need a pep talk. They were packing serious heat.

If it turned into a firefight, the old fortress was going to be outgunned.

All that mattered was getting his daughter back, no matter what the cost.

Her, and Dominique.

"Why don't we just go up there now and batter the fucking doors down?" one of the guests questioned. "That's the way your father would have done it."

"I am not my father," Danjuma said. "And as much as I loved him, he never had to worry about enemies having his children hostage. This is a new situation. We must use our heads."

There were nods and murmurs of approval.

"We wait at the shantytown until nightfall," Danjuma said. "Then we make our way out there. We won't be taking all the vehicles that close. The dust clouds would give us away long before engine sounds. It is a wasteland out there. Sound travels, dust clouds look out of place. These are not idiots we are dealing with. I'll go and join the people we've already got watching the old fortress. I'll message Rakeem when it's time for you to move in, but no one moves until I give the order. Is that clear?"

There were murmurs and nods of approval.

This was his call. They were the hammer in his hand.

"Do we have any idea how many of them there are in there?" The same old-timer asked. "That place can easily hold a couple of hundred men, maybe more."

"Have you been inside?" Danjuma asked, kicking himself for not thinking to ask if anyone had been inside sooner. Knowing the lay of the land could be the difference between life and a lot more deaths.

"Not since long before you were born," he said. "Some of us looted the place when it was first evacuated. We had a good look around. Of course, our own government put the army in there for a while after that, but they sealed everything up when they left."

"Can you remember anything about the place that might be of any help?"

The man shook his head. "Naw, I was barely knee-high, I just remember it was big, like a castle," he said. "There was some kind of walkway on the inside of the wall."

Danjuma nodded. "I've seen guards on it. During night watch there was only one up there most of the time. With luck, we catch them unaware, especially if our distraction on the inside pays off."

"Inside?"

He told them about the American and how he had taken Dominique inside with him. Soon they were all nodding among themselves, no more questions, no doubts.

The plan was coming together.

The next hour was spent in making sure everyone knew their roles, which cars they would be traveling in, and ensuring they were fully equipped.

There was a second room in the cellar, this one hidden behind a floor-to-ceiling wine rack. Behind it lay everything they could have needed and more. It was an armory. Danjuma had added to the arsenal, buying bigger and better, always hoping that it would serve as a deterrent that was never called upon. There was enough ordnance in that room to equip a small army, and that was exactly what walked out of the club that night.

CHAPTER
THIRTY-SIX

It was obvious they weren't used to entertaining guests.

If this was the special meal for guests, Dominique wondered what a normal mealtime usually looked like.

They had slaughtered a few chickens and thrown the meat into a heavily spiced broth along with some almost rotten vegetables. It was edible, barely, but it took a constant supply of beer to wash it down.

She was wary of the amount she drank, but Travis was drinking more than enough for both of them.

She was going to have to watch the idiot in case he started shooting his drunken mouth off.

Eventually the meal was over, but that didn't mean they were done in the mess hall; Boss and his men would be drinking until well into the night.

Dominique managed to drag Travis away when it was well on its way to midnight under the pretense of feeling horny. His acting was good enough that she wondered if the damned fool actually believed her.

Their departure drew a few jeers and plenty of leers, but no one really gave a shit about them slipping out.

And no one followed them.

It was a clear night, and desert cold.

Dominique slipped a denim jacket over her slinky dress. It was still chilly. She only noted four others out and about. Two of them were standing by a brazier, warming their hands and drinking something hot, the steam rose through the glow in front of their faces. Two more stood on the platform against the wall, near the gate. They stared out into the night, but not, she soon realized, with any sort of skilled vigilance. They were out of their depth here, playing at soldiers. She looped her arm through Travis', partly to guide him in the right direction, but mostly to make sure he stayed upright. She didn't want to have to deal with him sprawled out in the dirt.

Their car and been moved away from the gate.

That might make things a little more difficult in terms of being an extra complication, but nothing she couldn't deal with.

"Come on, lover boy," she said, a litter louder than she needed to.

It was enough for the men by the brazier to notice them. A couple whistled, one offered to take the American's place. Without making it obvious, she made sure that all of them had seen her and how she dressed. She didn't want them forgetting her.

The room they'd been given had a pair of bunks, a small table and a single chair, but very little else. Boss hadn't been lying, it was hardly Trump Towers, but she planned to spend as little time in it as possible. Right now, it was about putting everything in motion.

She drew the threadbare curtains.

As she turned back, the man wrapped his arms around her, one hand grabbing clumsily at her ass.

"Are we still playing the game?" he laughed.

It didn't take much to push him off. It took a lot more to refrain from hitting him so hard she knocked him out cold. She laughed it off and led him to the bottom bunk.

By the time she had opened her bag and laid out some of the clothes from it he was snoring.

She couldn't guarantee that it would stay that way when things kicked off, but she could hope. For his sake.

She slipped off the jacket and dropped it onto the back of the chair before peeling off the dress. She stood naked in the middle of the room. Travis snored on, blissfully ignorant. She dressed quickly in a pair of black jeans and a black hoodie that had been kept separate in the bag, beneath the false bottom and the brightly colored lingerie intended to distract whoever had searched it. It had worked. A pair of flat black pumps finished off the outfit. They weren't particularly sturdy, but they would be quiet, and stealthy was primary over the next few minutes.

All set, she had climbed onto the top bunk and waited, listening for signs of the party breaking up.

It was well after two before the place finally fell silent.

She allowed another twenty minutes before making her move. Danjuma had wanted a pre-arranged time but that would have been impossible. Put people in the mix and things became unpredictable. How long would it take them to get drunk? Would they have women in there to entertain them—or girls, knowing what they were trafficking? Would they sample the wares, and go high into the long night? With no way of knowing, and no way to reliably communicate with Danjuma she was about to make her move, she just had to take it on faith that he would be ready.

She trusted him.

What she couldn't trust was how quickly he could move when the shit hit the fan. The timings were going to be key to their success and getting Lori out of there alive.

Carefully, she opened the door and slipped out into the night.

Her first instinct was to start the distraction and then look for the girl, but if it went too fast and she couldn't locate her, then she died, and that wasn't going to happen. So, instead, she went in search of Lori, intending to keep her out of harm's way when the fireworks went off.

There was a stretch of near darkness that ran between the hut she had just come out of and the side wall of the compound. There, out of sight of anyone who might be moving about, she could get closer to the car when the time was right. She took a mental note and moved on. There were several windows on this side of the buildings. The sounds of snoring came from a few of the open ones. Sleeping quarters. Good to know. She tried to gauge how many men they might house and decided they couldn't all be in the same place. A glimpse across the courtyard, through the gap between buildings revealed a similar building on the opposite side of the compound.

A couple of other buildings were silent and refused to give up their secrets.

The sounds of movement came from the final building.

The windows were barred, the glass broken and packed with what might have been cardboard. Listening intently, she heard whispered voices coming from inside. Girls' voices. More than one.

Dominique thought about prepping them for what was to come but decided against it; the last thing she wanted to do was to excite them, as that would just create more noise, and maybe tip her hand too soon. They were as far from the gate as they possibly could be. That meant they were safe there, for now.

Confident that she had the lay of the land in her head, and a clear idea of where the danger would come from, she crept back along the same shadowy alleyway to the hut where Travis was still sound asleep.

It was only a matter of a dozen yards or so to the car they had arrived in. Now it was parked on the end of a row of other vehicles. She'd been hoping it would be left where she'd parked it, but beggars couldn't be choosers. She could still make it work. That was all that mattered.

Keeping low, she moved closer to the battered old car and placed a hand on the door handle, surprised to find it locked.

She'd prepared for even that eventuality.

She stretched out on the ground and slid underneath the car, gravel digging into her back through the material of the sweatshirt.

She shifted slowly, trying not to make the slightest sound, well aware that in reality she was making less noise than the crackle of wood in the brazier.

In the blackness she fumbled, her fingertips questing for her handiwork, until, at last, she found the magnetic box that held the spare key, and then the panel she'd cut out of the heat detectors and replaced with a larger piece of metal held in place by wing-nuts that were only finger-tight.

It was a slow and tortuous process, but eventually, she succeeded in removing the panel.

Out dropped a handgun and a knife wrapped in a towel.

If she'd told Danjuma what she was planning, he would have laughed her paranoia off, saying she was overcomplicating things, but she knew this was the best way. This way she had control. And that was important to her. She wasn't reliant upon anyone else. Her life was in her own hands. The weight of the gun felt good.

CHAPTER
THIRTY-SEVEN

Dana didn't know what to do with herself.

The house felt eerily silent because everyone had gone with her father to get her sister back.

She hated that it was her fault, and as much as she wanted to deny it or convince herself otherwise there was no escaping the truth, it was no one's fault but hers. She'd fallen for Lebna, she'd taken her to the apartment, she'd fucked up. And even at the last, if she'd let her sister out of the window first, she would have gotten away. Dana could have taken care of herself. She should have looked out for Lori; she was the older sister. None of this would have happened without her.

And yet she still found herself worrying about what Lebna had done, and where he had gone, because she was sure he hadn't cheated on her. That wasn't him. He loved her. She was his world.

A glance out of the window caught her by surprise; it was late.

She had no idea how much longer she'd have to wait for word from her father.

Her eyes felt tired and gritty, but there was no point in going to bed. There was no way she was going to sleep. Not until she knew what was happening. Part of her wished he'd never told her, so that she could have gone on in not-so blissful ignorance. But she knew, and because of that she worried about every tiny thing that might have gone wrong already, all the other tiny things that could still go wrong, and including that she could lose her father as well as her sister. Her spiraling thoughts were interrupted by the sound of something banging upstairs.

She'd forgotten about the American locked in the guest suite.

She had no idea if he'd been given anything to eat or drink since lunchtime, so she went up to check on him.

"You okay in there?" Dana asked as she tapped on the bedroom door.

The noise stopped, but he didn't answer her.

"What's the matter?" she asked, but without waiting for a response unlocked the door to find the man pacing the room like a caged tiger.

"What's going on?" He asked. "Where's Danjuma? I need to see him."

"He isn't here."

"Then where is he? I need to see him, or that other guy, Rakeem."

"Rakeem's not here either."

"I can't do this anymore. If he won't help me, I'd rather take my own chances."

"They've gone to get my sister back," she said, and as he stared at her, confused, the whole story started to pour out.

She told him about Lori being snatched, about the old army base, and the drug dealer that was going to help them get in there.

"I wanted to be there when they brought her out," she said. "I wanted to make sure she was okay," and then quieter, "because it's all my fault."

"Do you have a car?"

She nodded. "Dad bought it for me. Why...?" Eventually the penny dropped. "You think I should go? But I can't leave you here."

"I was thinking I could come with you. Moral support. That, and make sure you don't do anything stupid. Your dad trusts me. I'm a friend."

She didn't believe that, otherwise why the lock on the door? "I shouldn't even let you out of the room..."

"You're the one who said you wanted to be there, not me. I didn't put the idea in your head. It's all your idea. So, do you want to be there or not?"

"Of course I do," she said.

"Then let's go. I'll drive."

CHAPTER
THIRTY-EIGHT

Dominque opened the car door silently, grateful that the car was so old the keys were mechanical rather than electronic. No beeps to betray her. She'd removed the bulb from the overhead light to make sure that it wouldn't draw any attention as she got into the car.

She took a breath, wondering if she should have taken care of the guards before she did this. It was a calculated gamble; if she failed, she would lose any chance of getting Danjuma inside. This was about getting him in, no more, no less. At least not yet. Another breath and she started the engine, quickly reversing out of the space without turning the lights on.

She slipped the car into first gear and pressed the cigarette light into place. "One," she said and hit the accelerator, keeping the count going. "Two," the men at the brazier had turned to face her, surprise lit up on their face by the flames. No one reached for a weapon. "Three." The car picked up speed, hurtling towards the gate. She pushed the clutch and put the car into neutral. The car began to slow slightly, still moving forward. "Four." She opened the door and dived out, rolling away from the car as the first shot was fired. It was aimed at the car, not her. "Five."

The car exploded the moment before it hit the gate, but it was enough to destroy the metal bars, twisting them in a gout of flame as the engine exploded, showering debris in every direction.

Dominique scrambled away to shelter closer to the other vehicles. It wasn't the safest place to be as pieces of hot metal rained down, clattering down against the bodywork of the other cars, but it offered some protection. She dropped low, sliding under a jeep a heartbeat before the worst of it came crashing down, and rolled out the far side, ready to move again when the danger had passed.

She could see at last one body of the ground.

That meant there were three armed men out there looking for her.

In a few seconds they'd be joined by countless others, come to see what the fuck was going on. Men like this, their first impression would be that they were under attack. They wouldn't think the enemy was inside the walls. That was what she was banking on. She slipped the gun from the waistband of her jeans, ready to get a shot of her own.

Getting these three out of the way before others joined them would make it easier for Danjuma to get inside. She had no doubt they'd have brought plenty of firepower with them and be more than capable of dealing with any resistance Boss and his defenders could muster.

It took her a moment to see the two men on the raised platform.

One of them was spraying bullets wildly, barely in her general direction. He had no idea where she was. The other was trying to get down the ladder, but the blazing remains of the car were making it difficult.

The explosion had brought down the huge double gates, but the remains of the car were still burning in the gap, making it as effective a barrier as the iron gates had been. Danjuma would have to deal with it; there was nothing she could do about it without getting herself killed.

Her priority had to be staying alive.

Until they got there, at least.

The fourth man had been standing near the brazier. He'd moved to the side of a building, taking cover, but because he had no idea where she was, he'd left himself exposed.

He crept out into the open, gun held out in front of him like something out of a crappy movie, aiming in the same direction as the guard on the platform without a clue what he was supposed to be aiming at.

She could have taken him, but any shot from that position would give her away to the others, even if she took him out. But she wasn't about to lie there doing nothing until they found her. That wasn't how she worked.

She rolled out from under the Jeep. Keeping to the shadows between vehicles, she took a shot and ran, heading back into the alley between the bunk block and the wall without so much as pausing to see if she'd hit.

She reached the building where she'd left Travis snoring, and scrambled up onto the windowsill, then hauled herself up until she was on the sloping roof. The metal creaked impossibly loudly beneath her weight as she moved to the brace beam that supported the roof and spread herself flat upon it. Despite the noise she'd made, no one had noticed her climb. There was no one in her eye-line on the walkway.

As she watched, a handful of men stumbled out of the accommodation block. They were confused, pulling on clothes, with adrenalin pulsing through their veins. What she didn't see were weapons, which surprised her. Instinctively, she'd have gone for hers, that they didn't, said more about them and their sense of false security.

A glance in the direction of the gate, and she saw the car still blazing.

She also saw the man she'd taken a shot at, slumped on the ground.

He might not be dead, but he wasn't ok either.

Three down, maybe. That was something. But it wouldn't be long before the drunks realized the threat and responded in kind, collecting their weapons, and shooting at anything that moved.

By that time, there would be too many of them for her to make a difference.

Danjuma needed to get there quickly if she was going to get out of there alive, and even then she wasn't counting on it. Better she made sure the girl got away. She could do that for the man she loved.

She hadn't even thought about that word before, when it came to them.

And now was not the time to let emotion get in the way.

She had a job to do.

One of the men started to walk determinedly towards her, but the fool didn't look up once.

No doubt he was coming to check on the strangers. Their car was burning inside the gateway, after all.

There was no sign of Travis.

It was hard to imagine him sleeping through the chaos she'd unleashed, but the plan was for him to stay in place until she came looking for him.

She took a breath and took aim. The shout would betray her position but might be the difference for the American.

She gritted her teeth, steeling herself.

Her aim was true.

She wouldn't miss. Not from here.

She was about to pull the trigger when the air was filled with noise.

She pulled the trigger anyway.

CHAPTER
THIRTY-NINE

A jeep with sturdy bull bars charged into the burning wreckage of the car, slamming it backwards into the compound, and clearing space for three other vehicles to pile through behind it.

The ruined metal scraped against the ground, moving relentlessly.

Some of the defenders, roused from their beds and watched incredulously, a split second away from understanding. Then they ran out of the way before the twisted metal crushed them.

One stumbled, fell, tried to scramble to his feet but was too slow.

In an instant a dozen men bundled out of the vehicle, semi-automatics at the ready.

Danjuma's men were ruthless. They came to kill. They cut down anyone who didn't drop to the ground. Anyone with a weapon in their hand went to meet their god.

More men came running through the gateway, but by then it was as good as over.

The courtyard was lit up like it was day, with lights from the head-lights and halogen lamps, as well as the still blazing wreckage.

Danjuma had come prepared.

"Dominique!" Danjuma shouted, turning and turning again, trying to find her in the chaos.

"Up here," she said, indicating her presence without making any sudden moves.

"Have you found her?"

"I think so," she said, keeping the words between them to a mini-mum. She slipped back down the rear of the hut and scrambled down to the ground. She rushed around the bunk, pausing only to let Travis know it was safe to come out.

He was reluctant to move before he was sure it was all over.

A couple of guns were raised in her direction as she emerged from the shadows. Danjuma held out an arm and lowered it. She recognized some of the men around him, but not many.

He'd rounded up an army to bring his little girl home. She should have expected no less from him.

"Where?" He asked.

She nodded in the direction of the hut where she had heard the girl's voices, only to see a darker shadow where the door hung open.

Danjuma turned the beam of his torch inside, revealing easily twenty terrified young faces—painfully young, all of them girls. Some looked barely ten in the half-light, if that, others younger. What he knew instinctively, was that none of them were more than thirteen. That was the magic number. The realization made him feel sick.

But there was no sign of his daughter in there.

"Where is she?" he asked again, as if they were the only words he could get out.

Inside, the girls huddled closer together, holding onto each other like life rafts.

"He came for her," one said out of the shadows. "The new girl..."

And another repeated, "He came for her."

"Who did? Where did he take her?"

"Boss," the girl said.

"He can't have got far," Rakeem said, standing at Danjuma's shoulder.

Dominique agreed, "He couldn't have got out without us seeing him."

"So, then we tear the place apart brick by brick until we find him. And then we bury him under those bricks."

The search began, building by building, with increasing dread as they entered empty rooms and found nothing but junk, sometimes having to fight their way in only to find the defenders had been protecting nothing. The smell of blood and bullets was thick in the dusty air.

Gunfire rattled out, splitting the night outside the sound-dampening walls.

They found drunks, they found bodies, and eventually they found Boss.

He was in a room at the back of the kitchen, cornered like a rat, but he had a hostage—Lori—and a gun to her temple.

Boss had his ham hock of a forearm wrapped around his daughter's throat, she was pulled tight with no room to squirm free.

The girl was terrified. Vulnerable, she looked much younger than her age.

"Come any closer," the man said as Danjuma stepped inside the room, "And I'll pull the trigger."

"You don't want to do that."

"Fuck man, I don't want any of this. I don't have a fuckin' clue how we got here, this has all been some big fucking mistake."

He stared at Dominique in the doorway, appreciating how Danjuma had managed to get inside the compound.

"Give me my daughter," Danjuma said, the black eye of his own gun trained on Boss, though Dominque knew he would not pull the trigger; not while there was the slightest chance his daughter might take the hit.

"If you want her alive, you let me drive out of here."

"Like fuck do I do that," Danjuma shook his head. "You're in no position to bargain. Your men are dead or have surrendered and will be dead before dawn. There's you and only you. You make the mistake of hurting her, you join them. Let her go, then we can talk."

The men stared at each other. All was lost. Boss knew it. Danjuma waited. Eventually Boss relinquished his hold on the girl, and she scrambled to her feet, running to her father, who swept her up in a fierce embrace.

On his knees, Boss lowered his head, waiting for the execution. He spoke to the dirt. "This was all a mistake."

"So, you said," Danjuma said, into his daughter's hair.

"One of those idiot boys who work for me mistook her for the girlfriend of one of us. She was in the wrong place at the wrong time."

"Lebna's yours?" Danjuma asked.

Boss looked up. "He was. The idiots thought they could play detective and find out why the fuck you killed their friend."

"Me? I didn't kill anyone."

"Don't play dumb with me, man. I know you killed him, and if you're gonna pull that semantic shit and say you didn't do it yourself, you had him killed. The bit that grates though, why the fuck did you have to dump his body outside our gates in the middle of the fucking night? That's an act of war, man. We didn't come here for war. We came here for peace. And Lebna wound up dead. Some fucking price of peace."

"Lebna's dead?" a voice cried.

CHAPTER
FORTY

"Dana! What the ever-loving fuck are you doing here, girl?" Danjuma demanded, spinning around to face his eldest daughter.

"Because I couldn't stand waiting," she said, tears and dirt streaking her face.

"I don't... How? How did you know where to find us?"

"By listening at doors."

"Fuck. Fuck. Fuck. I *told* you to wait... I needed you to stay safe! And instead, you walk into the middle of a firefight on your own like some fucking mad woman wanting to get killed..."

"I'm not on my own," she said.

"Then who the fuck brought you here?"

"Connors."

"That fucking weasel?" Danjuma rasped. "Where is he? When I get my hands on him, I'll break his fucking neck for this."

She turned, confused. "He was behind me a moment ago."

"What did you tell him?"

"What?"

"How much does he know?"

Danjuma wanted to be angry with her, but that anger was more of a knotted ball in the pit of his stomach than any sort of fire. But this was all her fault. All of those bodies outside, they were on her, her dead to carry with her through her life. She was the one who'd put her sister's life at risk because she'd been so desperate to spread her legs for one of these men...

She shrugged. "I don't know... What does it matter?" The tears were streaming.

"It matters," Sol Danjuma said slowly, like he was explaining the ways of the world to a moron, "because the man who betrayed him is here."

"So?" she sobbed.

"Without him we wouldn't have gotten inside. We wouldn't have gotten your sister back. We do not want them finding each other... At least tell me Connors doesn't have a weapon?"

The answer in her eyes was not the one he'd been hoping for.

"Just... fuck this shit," he said, tired.

"I'll go," Dominique volunteered, turning without a moment of hesitation, and without waiting for him to agree. Not that she needed his permission; she wasn't one of his men.

He should have stopped her.

A better man would have sent someone else, but right then Danjuma wasn't a better man, he was a tired one, tired of fighting, tired of death.

She left, and that left him with the problem of two girls who shouldn't have been there. His girls. He wanted to put a bullet in the man's brain, but not in front of his girls. Could he believe a word that came out of the other man's mouth? He was talking to save his life—but that didn't make what he had to say true, did it?

But the possibility lingered; had Lori really been snatched by mistake? And if she had, why did Boss think he'd killed Lebna and dumped his body at their door?

"You and me, we need to talk," Danjuma said to the other man, and when Rakeem moved to join them, reaching to close the door, added, "Just you and me."

Rakeem started to protest, but Danjuma shook his head. "Look after the girls," he said. "I'm trusting you to get them home."

"But..."

"But nothing, Rakeem. There is honor in this. You are doing this for me. Now take his gun and get them out of here."

Rakeem huffed but grabbed the gun and ushered the two young women out of the makeshift cell.

Danjuma was sure that he muttered something as he departed but couldn't make it out. Perhaps that was for the best.

When they were gone, he closed the door. The room seemed smaller than ever. Claustrophobic.

"Tell me about Lebna," Danjuma said.

"What do you want to know?" Boss sniffed.

"Let's start with him being dead."

The man stared at him without blinking. "I watched his body burn on a funeral pyre," he said. "I watched his ashes being blown away."

"But what makes you think I had him killed?" Danjuma asked.

He listened as the man described the beat-up vehicle that had raced across the desert to their door and dumped the boy's body as if it was trash to be disposed of.

Danjuma let him finish before he told him, "It has nothing to do with me."

"Then who? Who else would want him dead?"

Danjuma shook his head.

He had almost shrugged but that would have been disrespectful. Not to the man in front of him, but to the young man his daughter loved.

"My daughter loved that boy. Why would I cause her pain?"

"There is no telling what a father will do," Boss said.

"And yet, here, in this moment I have no reason to lie to you. There is nothing to be gained from it. No angle. So, when I tell you I had nothing to do with the boy's death, you can take that to the bank."

Boss nodded. "I believe you."

"What did the vehicle look like?"

"I didn't see it, one of my boys did."

"Who?"

"Daudi. He's just a kid. He was a friend of Lebna's. They were tight."

"Is he here?"

"If he was smart enough to surrender. Otherwise you've already killed him," the man said.

Danjuma opened the door.

One of his men was lingering just a few feet away.

There was no sign of his daughters, or Rakeem.

"There's a boy out there, Daudi. Find him and bring him here."

The man took half a step, then paused as if expecting more instructions or some kind of explanation. When he didn't get either, he hurried away.

CHAPTER
FORTY-ONE

Out in the compound, the wreckage of the car still burned.

The blaze had started to die down, but still provided enough light to replace the headlights of cars. A couple of heads turned in Dominique's direction, but no one tried to stop her. There were bodies on the ground. She ignored them, going in search of the living. The defenders had been gathered together and were sitting with their hands on their heads, stripped of weapons and resistance. She didn't waste time on them. She had a single purpose; making sure Travis walked out of this place alive.

After that, he was on his own.

She felt alive again, as if something that had been hidden away for so long was coming back to light.

It occurred to her that perhaps walking this path again would change the future she had set up for herself, but there was nothing she could do about that.

All she could think about was that moment.

There was no sign of the man who had come with Danjuma's daughter. She didn't know if that was a mercy or not. Dominique couldn't imagine him being lucky enough to find Travis that quickly. But he would, eventually, because there were only so many places to look. Checking all the buildings trying to find him was a pointless exercise though, as he was almost certainly on the move, so she headed straight for the room she'd been sharing with Travis, thinking to protect him rather than hunt his ex-partner.

The bunk room was empty.

The blankets had been pushed back, a dent still in the pillow where his head had lain.

"Travis?" she whispered, and she heard the sound of movement, a shuffle beneath the bed, as the American eased himself out of his hiding place.

"Are we safe?" He asked.

"We found the girl," she said, but that wasn't an answer to his question. "But we have another problem."

Even in the dim light that managed to penetrate the room she could see that he was fully dressed; ready to move if he needed to. There was no hint that he'd spent most of the night drinking. Adrenalin could do that to a body. "What's up?"

"Your old partner," she said. "He's here, and he's not happy. Worse, for you, he knows you're here," she added, keeping her voice low.

"How?"

"Doesn't matter," Dominique said. "We need to get you out of here."

"He's going nowhere," said a voice from the doorway.

Dominique didn't need to turn to know who it was. "And you can drop the gun."

Travis was unarmed. She didn't think he was stupid enough to charge at the other man, not given the distance between them and the fact there was a gun aimed at him. Even if Connors was hesitant to fire, he'd still put a couple of bullets in his former friend before he was close enough to smell his sweat.

It was all down to her.

"Just toss it down there, lady, and you won't get hurt," Connors said, "I ain't got nothing against you. This is between me and my old friend here." And in that moment, she knew he was there for the taking. It gave her an edge. It gave her possibilities.

"Over there?" she asked, making her grip on the weapon seem uncertain in the sliver of light that came in through the open doorway.

"Sure."

"Won't it go off if I throw it?"

"Come on, lady. Don't be a wise-ass, just do it."

She watched his eyes follow her hand as she drew it back then threw the gun towards the wall. At the instant she released it, in the moment that he glanced away to see where the gun was going to land, she swung with her other fist, connecting brutally with the side of his jaw. The blow sent him stumbling back.

She chopped at the hand that held his gun, springing his grip, just as her right connected with his groin.

Hard.

He doubled up.

She had no need for a killing blow. This was a recovery, not a hit. "Come on, move."

Travis didn't need telling twice.

He was on his feet with the bag of cash in hand. He wasn't giving that up, even with a gun to the head. He started to run, and if he was smart, he would be well on his way to the border before looking back.

She picked up the two guns and spared the other American, on his knees now, one last glance. He wasn't going anywhere in a hurry. Even so, she crouched down beside him and said, "If I were you, I'd stay here for a while. You go back out there; I can't promise you that you won't get shot." There was no need to do or say more than that. Connors was a lot of things, but primarily he was a coward, and without his gun he reverted to the type.

Travis waited for her just outside the door, hugging close to the building. He knew that he was going to need her help to get out of there. He followed where she led.

Dominique waved to one of the men she recognized as she made her way to the line of parked cars and vans. A glance inside showed that the keys were already in the ignition. "You're driving," she told Travis. Danjuma's man didn't challenge her as Travis slid into the driver's seat. He threw the cash in the back. She didn't join him.

"They're not going to shoot me as I drive away, are they?"

"They might," she grinned, then when she realized he couldn't tell she was joking, said, "No. You're good to go. No one's going to come after you. Go before someone changes their mind. The border's that way," she pointed out towards the open road and banged twice on the side of the door to send him on his way.

He gunned the engine into life and backed it out of the space before turning towards the gateway.

The glow from the wreckage exposed several bullet holes and a shattered rear window, but there was no real damage that would prevent him from getting far, far away.

She stood in the gateway and watched the car's taillights until the American reached the end of the track and turned left towards the border.

He was no longer her responsibility.

She'd done everything she needed to do.

For once, she had saved a life.

It felt good.

After having a quick word with another of Danjuma's men, informing him about the other American in the bunk room, and making sure he understood it was for the best that he stayed there, she headed back to see if there was anything else she could do.

A battered white truck pulled away as she approached the building.

She caught a glimpse of Danjuma's daughters inside.

They didn't look particularly happy, but the eldest raised a hand in her direction. She watched as the truck worked its way around the wreckage, revealing a broken taillight before it too went through the gates and was gone.

CHAPTER
FORTY-TWO

"Is this him?" Danjuma demanded when the boy appeared in the doorway.

He was young, pathetically so, given how much trouble he'd caused. To Danjuma's eye, he looked as though he'd barely started to shave. The fear in his eyes was unmistakable.

Boss nodded. "This is our idiot, Daudi M'Beki," he said. "Tell him everything, Daudi. He won't hurt you. You have my word."

Danjuma couldn't help but raise an eyebrow at the promise the man had no right to give, but let it pass. "What happened the night Lebna came back?"

The boy's eyes flickered to Boss who simply nodded. "He didn't come back. He was already dead," the boy answered, finding his courage. "There was nothing we could do for him. Not that anyone tried."

"Then tell me, how did his body come back?"

"There was a truck. It came racing up the desert road from the shantytown, coming in the direction of Freetown. It came like the devil himself was chasing it. They pushed his body out and left him in the dirt."

Danjuma nodded. A truck. That was very little help, with there being hundreds if not thousands of them littering the streets of Freetown. "Did you get a look at the driver?"

Daudi shook his head. "It was dark, middle of the night watch. I wasn't even sure that it was a body until I got close to it. At first, I'd thought it was a bomb... That someone was attacking us."

Again, Danjuma nodded. Boss said nothing. "Where were you when you saw it? In the fields?"

"Nah, there's a walkway, on the inside of the wall."

"Alone?" Danjuma asked

The boy nodded, a little reluctantly, and glanced at Boss.

Danjuma grunted.

He'd seen first-hand the operation wasn't as tight as it should have been. The walls offered the illusion of safety, but the place was far from secure. In the end, they'd just driven through the front door.

With a little help, of course.

"Tell me about the vehicle?" he pushed. It was their only lead.

The boy shrugged. "Like I said, it was dark. I can't even be sure what color it was."

"Guess."

Danjuma was sure he was telling the truth; he had no reason to lie, but there had to be something, some detail, something that might help him put a name on the murderer working in his town.

"There was one thing," Daudi said, as though suddenly remembering something, some little detail that he hadn't realized he'd seen.

Danjuma waited, doing his best to stay calm. Let the boy find the memory. It was too important to rush.

"It had a broken taillight. Passenger side. I saw it after it pulled a U-turn and powered away."

The boy beamed at Danjuma, hoping he'd managed to give him something important.

A busted taillight.

There had to be dozens of vehicles with broken taillights, maybe even hundreds. How many trucks? Too many. Truth was, no one cared about busted lights, not the drivers, not what passed for local law enforcement, which was a pitiful thing at the best of times. The only thing they gave a fuck about was that people weren't killing each other, and even then, it was hard for them to really care beyond how it put them out. Traffic violations were way down their list of priorities.

"Thanks," Danjuma said. "But I don't know that it helps. A truck with a busted light. If that's all you can tell me though, you might as well go."

The boy nodded, but the smile faded to a line of straight lips. "Sorry," he said.

"Not your fault," Danjuma said.

"What now," said Boss after the boy had gone. "You doing to kill us all?"

"Is that what you would do?"

The man shrugged. "Who knows? If I'm being honest, maybe."

"And that was the same kid who brought my daughter here?"

Boss nodded. "It was. He panicked. I'd told him to stay out of town, but they didn't listen. He wanted to know what had happened to his friend. They fucked up, now we've paid the price of them panicking."

"But he wasn't the one who'd decided to sell her into the sex slave trade, though, was he? That was you. And it's harder to forgive that as some panicked mistake. That was cold. Calculated. You made a decision. Maybe it was one of expedience, maybe it's just what you do, I mean, that's what it looks like to me. Why else would you have so many kids here? You're no better than a fucking pimp. No, you're worse, because they're fucking kids, man. Kids. You're a sick fuck. I'd be doing the world a favor if I ended you. That's what I think."

The man said nothing, but Danjuma knew that he had a decision to make, though in truth he'd already made it. He didn't have a problem with people dealing drugs, how could he? He wasn't a hypocrite. He didn't give a shit about betrayal, back-stabbing or any other bullshit. It was all stock in his own trade. He wasn't keen on the idea of a rival on his doorstep, but the man's strength was broken. He wasn't going to be fighting for Freetown any time soon. All of those things could have been forgiven. Deals could have been struck. But he drew the line at buying and selling kids.

Especially when one of them had been his own.

"What would you have done if you had been in my place?" Boss asked. "Be honest. You'd have done the same."

"That's where you're wrong," Danjuma said. In a way their places had been reversed. Just as Boss had made a decision about Danjuma's daughter, Danjuma made a decision about the fate of the man who called himself Boss. It wasn't some great dilemma, primarily because the difference in situations was stark; she was innocent while this man wasn't.

Danjuma executed him.

One shot.

To the head.

CHAPTER
FORTY-THREE

Dominique heard the shot before she reached the building.

She quickened her pace, heart suddenly racing.

She was sure that Boss was unarmed, Danjuma wasn't a fool. He would have patted him down even after he'd disarmed him, but that didn't stop her from feeling that single moment of pure terror where the only thing that existed was the possibility, what if?

She drew her own weapon before she entered, moving fast, center of gravity low, keeping close to the wall.

She needn't have worried.

She saw the open doorway.

Danjuma filled the space his arms limp at his side, still holding his own piece.

There was a new corpse on the floor behind him.

"Sol," she said softly, not wanting to startle him.

She knew what people were capable of in the moments after killing. It was a special time.

He didn't turn for a moment.

When he did, it was slowly.

She saw more of the dead Boss in that moment than she wanted to, including the exit wound and his blood sprayed across the wall behind him.

"You good?"

"I'm good," Danjuma said.

"What did the boy have to say? Did he know anything we can use?"

"Not much. He didn't get a look at the driver. All he could tell me was that it was a battered old truck, and it had a busted taillight. He couldn't even tell me what kind of truck it was."

"A busted taillight? Passenger side?" she said, a silent alarm tripping in her subconscious mind.

Danjuma nodded.

She slipped her weapon back into the waistband of her jeans. "We have to go. Now."

"What?"

"No questions. We just have to go. Trust me."

She turned away from him and was moving out of the building, fast. She didn't bother to glance back to see if he was following. There wasn't time to explain now; she'd tell him what she knew when they were moving.

Maybe she was wrong.

Maybe there wasn't a chance that they'd delivered his daughter into real danger thinking they were sending her home, safe. Dominique wasn't prepared to take that chance.

Not when the man behind the wheel was Rakeem.

Outside, she spotted the jeep that some of Danjuma's men had arrived in. It was a good all-terrain vehicle. She headed straight for it. The car she'd come in was a smoking ruin now, still releasing its noxious fumes. It had done its job and done it well.

She was relieved to find the keys in the ignition, as with the other cars, but she didn't need them. She could have hot-wired it faster than most people could turn the ignition.

She jumped into the driver's seat and gunned the engine into life before Danjuma was in the passenger seat.

"What the fuck is going on?" He demanded as she peeled away, tires spitting dust and gravel. There was blood in the spray, but that was the last thing on her mind as she put her foot down. Danjuma was thrown sideways as she slewed, aiming for the gateway, and grabbed the roll-bar to stop himself from falling out. A heartbeat later she swerved around the smoldering remains and was out through the gate.

With her foot flat to the floor, the engine screamed as the jeep careened through the narrow gap, the passenger side mirror catching on the stone pillar and snapping off with a wrenching scream of twisted metal.

"You want me to drive?" Danjuma shouted above the roar of the engine.

"You won't get us there any quicker," Dominique said, eyes front.

"No, but I might get us there alive," he said. "Wherever there is."

They were already almost at the end of the rutted lane at the fork that led back to Freetown or the border. She didn't brake until the last possible moment, throwing the car to the right to take the turn towards the shantytown and the city beyond.

"Time to tell me what the fuck is going on, Dom, and I'm not fucking joking."

"I know who killed your daughter's boyfriend."

"Who?"

"You know who. I've no idea why, but trust me, you know, and you know it makes sense."

"Who?" Danjuma said again.

"Rakeem," she said calmly, glancing across at him to gauge his reaction.

"Are you out of your mind?"

"I saw the busted taillight on his truck," Dominique said.

"So what? There are a thousand trucks in this place with busted taillights, like I told the kid, that doesn't mean anything."

"You're blind. I get it. Friendship does that. Loyalty. You didn't see the way he looked at the girls when you told him to take them home."

"But I've known him for years… He wouldn't…"

"What difference does that make? Ask yourself, who knew where the boy was from?"

The answer was, "Rakeem."

"And who was watching him for you?"

Again, the answer was, "Rakeem."

"So, means, opportunity, who else would have been able to kill him without Rakeem seeing and reporting back to you?" He said nothing. "Who would have known where to drop the body if he wanted to start a war?"

Again, Danjuma didn't answer. But his mind was racing. Why would Rakeem want a war?

To be the king, you have to kill the king.

That was something his father used to say.

Was that it?

He pulled out his phone.

She wasn't sure who he was calling.

"Keep them there until I get back," he said into the handset. "Make sure those little girls are okay. I'll be back as soon as I can." Without waiting for a response, he hung up then released a heavy sigh.

"I thought you were gonna call the girls, try to warn them."

"What good would that do? And if you're right, then well, they're not actresses. They're not built to lie. No, that would have just put them on edge and pushed him over it. But again, that's a big fucking if," but he didn't seem to be trying to convince himself anymore.

The sky was slowly growing lighter.

In the distance Dominique could just make out a single red light.

CHAPTER
FORTY-FOUR

"What do you think dad will do with them all?" Dana asked. Then she answered herself. "I don't want to know... he sent us away... he didn't do that because he was going to let them go."

Her little sister looked at her like she'd just said their father was a monster. "He wouldn't do something like... what you're not saying... Besides, and I shouldn't be telling you this, but I think I like the boy who took me there."

"Like him? He kidnapped you!"

"But he didn't mean to."

"Well, he hardly did it by accident."

"He thought he was kidnapping *you*," she said. "He didn't even know I existed."

"You've lost me," Dana said.

"It's simple enough. He was looking for Lebna's girlfriend. You, not me."

"So why was he looking for me?"

"To try to find out who killed him. They were friends. Brothers. They went through a lot escaping their homeland. They got here; they were finally safe. Then someone murdered Lebna."

"I still can't get my head around him being dead," Dana said, but there were no tears this time. "I don't understand though, who wanted to kill him if it wasn't one of those men?"

Her sister shrugged and stared into the darkness outside the car.

In the distance the sky had begun lightening, only a little, it would still be some time before they actually saw the sun.

"What do you think, Uncle Rakeem?" she asked then. "You must have an idea?"

"Who knows," Rakeem said, "They're scum. They're not like us. Plenty of people want them gone, back over the border where they came from. They don't belong here. None of them. They're not good people." He kept his eyes on the road ahead, not once glancing towards her. It felt odd, the three of them sitting on the bench seat in the front. Although it was intended to carry three, it felt a little too tightly packed, though neither she nor her sister were particularly big.

She could feel the heat of Rakeem's legs through her own jeans.

It made her feel uncomfortable.

She tried to inch away from him without drawing attention to it.

"He wasn't good enough for you," the man she called uncle said eventually. "That boy. He wasn't good enough. You deserve someone better than him."

"What makes you say that, Uncle?"

"Because once I knew he was part of that gang... and I knew what they did... trafficking young girls... I just knew... he wasn't good." Not good enough this time, she noticed, just not good.

"He'd left them," Dana said. "That was why he had the apartment in town. He wasn't part of that. It might not have been much, but it was going to be our home."

Rakeem snorted. "Not good enough," he said. "The boy was trash. He went back to where he belonged."

She let that settle, not liking where the insinuation was leading her mind.

"So," she said sweetly, after a moment, "Who *do* you think is good enough for me?" She let that dangle there for a moment, before she asked, "You?"

She twisted slightly in her seat, sure that a blush came to his cheeks in the dim green light of the dashboard.

"Why not?" he snarled. "Why wouldn't I be good enough for the precious Dana Danjuma?"

Dana laughed, unable to stop herself. "But you're Uncle Rakeem," she said realizing he was serious.

Then the other shoe dropped.

And for a moment the world seemed to stand still.

"You did it," she said then, knowing she was right. "You killed him. You killed him because you didn't want us to be together." And beneath it, the understanding that he thought that for as long as she was on her own, he had a chance to lay claim to her. Do some sort of deal with her father. Get her as a reward for his loyal service. She felt sick. "Well, let me tell you something. You'd have never had a chance, even if dad had made me, even if you were the last man on earth, I still wouldn't *want* to be with you. I'd rather be dead. Now stop that car. We can walk the rest of the way."

"Don't be silly. We're in the middle of nowhere."

"I don't care. I'd rather walk than spend a moment longer in here with you. Stop the truck!" she screamed, but he kept driving, their speed increasing. "Stop the fucking truck," she screamed again, and when he failed to acknowledge her, she clawed at his face, trying to gouge at his eyes with sharp nails.

He shrugged her away, throwing his arm to keep her at bay.

Then the truck's cabin was filled with light. Blinding. Bright.

It took her a moment to realize it was from the headlights and halogen lamps of the jeep behind them. It was brighter than sunshine.

"Stop this fucking van!" Dana screamed again, then without thinking, grabbed at the handbrake, and yanked back on it, hard.

The truck shrieked, then a heartbeat later she was stuck inside a metal box, rolling and tumbling, the world full of agony and sound, of twisting metals and screams.

And then there was a moment of silence, but everything inside it felt wrong.

Only the seatbelt had saved her.

She couldn't move.

She wasn't sure if it was because she was trapped, or because her mind wouldn't let her body respond with the fear coursing through her limbs.

"Sis?" she called out, not daring to hope Lori would answer, but needing her to.

There was a groan in response.

That was enough.

For the moment, at least.

She tried to turn, frightened to see what Rakeem was doing, imagining him clawing at his seatbelt to get out and at her, only to see him wedged at an awkward angle against the door. His head was twisted. She saw a bone pressing out against his neck. She couldn't tell if he was breathing, and in that moment she didn't care.

There was something warm and wet on her cheek.

She couldn't tell if it was tears or blood.

She wanted to close her eyes.

She wanted to sleep.

To escape the pain.

And then one of the doors screeched open.

CHAPTER 45

Six Months Later

"It's a wonderful thing what you're doing," Dominique said, her arm linked in Sol Danjuma's as she leaned into him. "You're making a difference to these people."

"You're making me soft in my old age," he laughed enjoying her nearness. "You're a bad influence." But he liked the feeling this place gave him. It felt good to be doing something good. It had taken a while to clean up the old military base, but it had been transformed.

The day after what could have turned into a war but ended so differently because of the woman standing next to him, Danjuma had returned to the site of the slaughter to find that he'd been mistaken—there had been shots, and yes, some had fallen, but only a handful. Most of the defenders had surrendered. He hadn't lost a soul from his own men.

He'd been happy to allow the defenders the dignity of burning their dead, as was their custom, but after they had done that, they'd been lost, leaderless. He had offered them the choice; leave, go back over the border to the homeland they had abandoned and take their chances there, or stay here and try to build something new.

Most of the Awon Woli had chosen to stay.

Thankfully, his girls had suffered little more than a few cuts and bruises that healed a lot faster than the trauma Rakeem's betrayals had done to their minds. He had to smile at the way they fussed at the tiniest scratches on their skin. He told them scars were things of beauty because only survivors carried scars, but they weren't buying it.

Dana had refused to come out to this place again, but her sister was in the thick of things, full of ideas as to what should be done with the place.

He wasn't a psychologist, but he was smart enough in terms of people and the way they acted, to know she was doing it as a form of exorcism. She was banishing the ghosts of this place, her dead, even though he knew she would carry them with her for the rest of her days. What was obvious though, was that she enjoyed being around the boy, Daudi M'Beki. Not that it was going to be some fairy tale ending for them. It was more like a broken bird thing, with her wanting to fix him before she sent him off into the world. Danjuma could live with that. For now.

Even so, it was hard to trust that his girls were growing up twice as smart as he'd ever been. But then they took after their mother.

Rakeem.

The betrayal stung.

It had taken Dominique to tease the full extent of it out of Dana, but more than once she had found Rakeem following her, turning up in unexpected places. She'd mistakenly thought that he'd ordered his man to shadow her and had shrugged it off as more overly protective parental intrusion.

But then she had seen the way he looked at her in the truck and she'd known.

"He was infatuated with her," Dominique explained. "He probably thought you'd give her to him, a gift, keeping it in the family, cementing his place at your side, good old Uncle Rakeem..."

He was only ten years older than her, he thought. *Was.* Of course, he wouldn't get any older.

When the truck had rolled, he hadn't been wearing a seatbelt, unlike the girls. That had saved them. He had broken his neck and was dead before Danjuma had dragged his girls out of there.

He could have tried to get the body out of the truck, but in that moment, he realized the Awon Woli had the right idea when it came to their dead. He had put a light to the gas tank and stepped back, watching the bastard who had so very nearly cost him everything burn.

"You can't blame yourself."

"That's easy to say."

"The girls don't blame you, even though they know what you asked him to do. They know you did it because you love them."

"And what do I do about this one?" he asked pointing across at Daudi who was laughing as he shared a bottle of water with his youngest daughter. They looked happy together. Painfully so. But she was young; too young.

"Sometimes you just have to let them make their own mistakes. But I'll keep an eye on her. She seems to like me."

"They both do," he said and grinned. "And with good reason. It's me they're not too fond of right now, mainly for keeping you hidden."

"Well, that's on both of us," she said. "Not just you. Leave it to me. I speak teenage girl. I'll go and see if she's ready to head back with us to grab some lunch."

Danjuma watched as the woman walked away from him, all lithe and sinuous. He had worried things would change when he'd seen what she was capable of. Maybe they had, but only for the better. She was one of a kind.

The old base no longer served as a base of operations for drug runners and people smugglers, even though some of them remained.

The huts had been turned into living spaces and a few extra buildings had been added, nothing special, but safe, and that was what was important. Now they housed family after family of refugees. The place had a generator and a well that provided clean water, and outside the walls, a patch of land was being cultivated. It was already home.

Most of the young girls had stayed, too.

One or two had come from villages not too far away, and Danjuma had promised to see they got back home. A few of the others had been taken in by some of the families who had lost children of their own or had girls of similar ages. A handful of others chose to remain here, together, turning the room that had been their prison into a fresh start.

Sol Danjuma didn't know what had happened to the other American, or the four blocks of cocaine that had brought him here in the first place. He knew that Travis had left with the cash he had been promised, so most likely Connors had gotten the bricks of coke and they'd both left with what they came for after all.

They'd found Boss's safe.

One of Danjuma's men had blown it open.

There was money in there. A lot of it. But Sol Danjuma wasn't a thief. He didn't need the dead man's money. Instead, he offered it to those of Boss's men who'd chosen to remain, and they had decided that it would be better used towards the work they were doing in exchange for a place in it for themselves.

A fresh start.

A safe haven.

Danjuma could hardly refuse.

He watched Dominique walking towards him, her arm around his daughter's shoulder. They were chattering away like the oldest and best of friends. She was exactly what Dana needed. Danjuma knew that everything would be alright. Things were changing, yes, but sometimes change was for the best.

THE END

KINGSTON IMPERIAL

Marvis Johnson — Publisher
Joshua Wirth — Designer
Roby Marcondes — Marketing Manager

Contact:
Kingston Imperial
144 North 7th Street #255
Brooklyn, NY 11249
Email: Info@kingstonimperial.com
www.kingstonimperial.com